WHAT *is* LEFT OVER AFTER

WHAT *is* LEFT OVER AFTER
NATASHA LESTER

FREMANTLE PRESS

Natasha Lester worked as a marketing executive for L'Oreal before turning her hand to writing. She won the Hungerford Award for her first novel *What is Left Over After*. Since then, she's become a New York Times–bestselling author of seven historical novels, including *The French Photographer*, *The Paris Secret*, *The Riviera House*, and *The Three Lives of Alix St Pierre*. Her books have been translated into many different languages and are published all around the world. When she's not writing, she loves collecting vintage fashion and practising the art of fashion illustration. Natasha lives with her husband and three children in Perth, Western Australia.

natashalester.com.au

Book club notes available from
fremantlepress.com.au

To Russell, for always believing

With you I could have
more than one skin,
a blank interior, a repertoire
of untold stories,
a fresh beginning.

MARGARET ATWOOD

PROLOGUE

It is nearly midnight and I have circled this room a hundred times. I stop. Rub my stomach. Nothing. Prod. Still nothing. I lift my shirt and watch the pearl of my belly in the mirror. It does not move. I sit, then stand.

I resort to the camera for company but when I pick it up and study the lens it does not soothe the worry I am unable to define. The photographs of my family, hung on the wall, attract my wandering eyes, my wandering fingers. I pass my hand over Pépé's and bring it to rest on Jason's heart. Then I know. The baby has been too still for too long. The camera cracks to the floor.

ﱞ

'Let's lie you down here.' The midwife helps me onto a bed and then asks, 'How many weeks?'

'Thirty-six,' I say.

'First-time mum?'

'Yes. Sorry to bother you. But she's normally so active. I thought I should check.'

The midwife nods and smiles as if indulging a child. I know she does not believe me, that she thinks I'm worrying over nothing. She leaves and I stare at the room. Stark fluorescents render everything flat, caricatured. Bleached walls and floors shimmer like glass.

The midwife returns and straps a band around my belly, sticks two discs on my skin and connects the baby, through me, to a machine. A slow thud begins to sound and the machine disgorges a stream of paper, printed with lines and dots. I want to study the markings but I'm distracted by the sluggish thumping sound that is loud, so loud. Why are they monitoring my heartbeat? Where is the rapid series of eighth notes that make up my baby's heartbeat?

I see it then, a flicker of uncertainty that erases the midwife's habitual smile.

'What?' I ask.

'Just a minute.' She disappears.

I am left coupled to a machine, ears too full of that slow, slow throb, hand grasping at paper I cannot read, wondering how the shapes made by a robotic pencil can possibly signify my baby.

A doctor comes in; he moves like Jason, urgently but with assurance. He asks me the same questions that the midwife has already asked, as if trying to find a falsehood in my story. I give him the same answers but my voice does not sound the same.

He looks at the paper and listens, as if to the baby.

I wonder what she says. Does she cry out, Help!

'Where's your husband?' the doctor asks.

'At work. He's a surgeon.'

The doctor turns to the midwife. 'Get him.' Then he turns back to me. 'You need an emergency caesar.'

'No. She's not ready. I'm not ready. I don't have my bag. I left it at home. All the things I'm supposed to bring. I have nothing.'

'The baby is distressed,' the doctor says. 'Its heart rate is too low.'

Its heart rate. Not my heart rate then.

Wheeling away. Fast. Too fast.

PART I

ONE

This story really begins at midnight one month after Aurora was born, the night of her due date, the night she couldn't wait for, such was her wish to rush headfirst into our lives.

I managed to arrive home just before Jason. I heard him come through the door and drop his keys on the walnut chiffonier, even though he knew I hated the way the metal scratched its polished surface. He almost fell into the sofa and then placed his hand on his right temple, pressing his pulse point as if the pain of blood pumping through his skull was too much to bear. In that gesture, I could see his failure. The heart he couldn't save. The heart that became flaccid in his surgeon's hands as a life passed through his operating theatre.

I shifted on the sofa opposite and his hand fell to his knee.

'Shit Gaelle, what are you doing in the dark? I thought you were in bed.'

'I couldn't sleep.'

He closed his eyes and in the silence I could almost hear a tear form in the corner of his eye, hear the pop as the surface tension broke and it slipped over his face.

'You left early this morning,' I said.

'I went for a dive with Gus.'

'Where did you go?'

'Fairy Bower.'

'What did you see?'

'Fish, Gaelle. Fish and coral.'

'Did you take any photos?'

'I didn't take the camera. It gets in the way. You have this crazy idea that I'm into photography because I've kept my old photo albums. The albums were just somewhere to put stuff. They were storage.'

I stood up, shivering. Jason had left the front door open and the breeze was pushing in and all I was wearing was a dress of transparent chiffon. No cardigan. No shoes. No underwear.

I picked up the photograph of the three of us that sat on the dresser beside Aurora's silver Tiffany rattle. 'What about this, Jason? Is this storage too? Do you just put us in a frame and then go off to work and think about hearts?'

'I dreamed about Aurora last night.'

I walked away.

But he followed and continued to talk, like a high school girl babbling about her latest crush. 'She'd grown up. She was about six and she was running away from me and smiling. Her smile was beautiful.'

'Was I in your dream too?'

He did not answer with his voice. The answer sat between his eyes and mine, which were locked together, seeing what there was left to see, of us. What Aurora had not taken for herself. What we had not given over to her. And that was why I found his hand, directed his body against the wall and searched his mouth with mine.

I had kissed another man earlier that night and I wondered if Jason could taste this, whether he could tell that my lips had travelled the length of another man's back, whether sweat and sex were still there, corroding my tongue. I'd screwed the man whilst fully clothed; the clouds had curtained the stars and all I could see as I stood on his balcony were the stains left by boat lights on the water at Rose Bay and then I could see only the dark because I closed my eyes as I felt the man step up behind me, slide his hands beneath my dress and circle my skin through the silk of my knickers. Then my knickers were pushed down and the man's penis was inside me and his fingers were not circling any more but pressing hard against my skin and I thought I could feel someone watching so I opened my eyes but before I could see whether the shadow on the balcony opposite was a person or a pot plant the man came and then I could see nothing because it was time to go home.

But the sex I needed to have now with my husband was the naked sort. I needed to take off my clothes, take off Jason's clothes. If I could place all my skin alongside all his skin then the chill would go away. If we could both be undone by one another in the way that we used to be before Aurora was born then I would stop.

So I opened Jason's shirt and tossed off my dress. Our arms curled around one another's backs and I could feel the warmth begin. But then I saw, in the slight light cast by the street, a blemish, like a scar, sitting next to his left nipple, resting between his ribs. As his fingers carved a line down my back, I wondered why I had never noticed the scar before. I traced its outline and Jason's hands moved to my buttocks, holding me close as if he was searching for something too. More flesh, perhaps. Or flesh speaking.

I wanted to taste the scar, wanted to roll it across my tongue and make it shine like silver. So I pulled him down to the floor, pressed his back along the cold marble, and lifted my hips over his. Then I lowered my lips towards his chest and paused—all I wanted was for us to stay like that, my mouth open, ready to taste the thick skin of a healed wound.

But then I saw his penis, resting against his groin, as flaccid as the dead heart. He turned his body away from me, away from the light, so that I could not see his face at all when he said sorry.

TWO

I found out that I was pregnant again about one month later, the night we restarted our Friday night dinners with Jason's friends and their wives. Our friends, Jason would always say when I described them as such. But this was a group of people who had been friends and lovers since university and for whom, as far as I could see, longevity was one of the primary reasons they were all still together. The men were stockbrokers, doctors and investment bankers and I knew which person had which label and which wife and which children but I did not know which person had seen a marriage counsellor and which person had cried when their daughter had a febrile convulsion and which person played the piano at night when everybody else was sleeping.

The women were mothers, either full-time or part-time, and I could not tell whether I looked down more on the ones who stayed home to raise their children or the ones who left their children in day care to go back to work and spend two or three days trying to finish five days' work, never complaining because they did not want anyone to think that motherhood had rendered them incompetent.

I always invited Imogen and her husband to these dinners because, even though Imogen left her two children with a nanny three days a week to return to her job as a beauty editor for a teen magazine, I could never look down on someone who was the first friend I ever had.

I found myself stuck in the kitchen on the Friday afternoon making cassoulet for the dinner party, remembering how Jason had said he would organise it. I wouldn't even have to cook; he'd order in. Having everyone over as we used to, before Aurora, would help us get back into a routine. All the books and all the people we'd spoken to had said this was important. I was thinking about this and the sushi he'd forgotten to order and the ingredients for the cassoulet, which took several hours and required my full attention, so I did not answer Jason straight away when he said, 'I think we should move Aurora's cradle out of our room.'

Three months. We'd agreed before she was born that we would have the cradle in our room for three months. Only two months had passed. I continued to cut the salted belly of pork into four pieces, ready to add to the lingots boiling on the stove. But Jason stepped over to me, took my shoulders in his hands, swivelled my body away from the chopping block, tilted my chin up and said again, 'Gaelle, we need to move the cradle out of our room.'

My eyes were pointed in his direction but they did not see him; instead they saw me, my Hermès scarf knotted around my throat, my lips painted crimson and my hand wrapped around a Laguiole knife, slippery with pork fat. My mind was running through the recipe—heating duck fat, frying sausages—but I'd forgotten to buy the Toulouse sausages the dish required and the barbecue sausages in our freezer were not up to the demands of a cassoulet. I put down the knife, picked up my keys and said, 'I have to go and buy sausage.'

'The sausage can wait,' Jason said.

'No it can't. It's two o'clock already. Dinner's going to be late.'

'No one will care. We can still order sushi.'

'I will care. And I don't feel like sushi.'

'What about the cradle?' He plucked the keys from my hand and I grabbed at them like a child snatching lollies. But he was bigger, stronger.

'There is no timeline or flow chart, Jason. We don't always have to move on to the next step in whatever baby process you've created inside your head.'

I'd wanted to say this to Jason since we came back from the hospital; every time I sat in the breastfeeding chair in Aurora's room and watched him put away the summer clothes because we wouldn't need them in such a cold spring or store the massage oil that was too strong and made the whole room smell like fresh baby, I wanted to say, *Stop. Leave everything how it is. I'm her mother. I will know when it's the right time to put those things away.* Instead I would wait until he went to work and then I would go into the room and take the things out of the storage box and put them back onto shelves and into drawers. Massage helped babies sleep; sometimes there were hot days in spring, and the risk of SIDS was lower if the baby slept in the mother's room. I knew these facts. I knew we shouldn't put anything away.

Jason looked at me then and he did not see the mother who knew that nothing should be put away; he saw his wife with a knife in her hand and another quarrel clattering from her mouth. And so I did not see that behind his processes and timelines and flow charts there might be some other knowledge about Aurora, some other understanding. 'Fine, I'll move the cradle,' I said. 'When I get back from the shop.'

'I'll do it while you're out.'

'No.'

We were standing on either side of the island bench. I was gripping the marble top. Jason was too. But then he lifted his hand, stretched it out and laid it on mine. 'Ellie, we have to move the cradle some time. If we do it together, it might be easier.'

I pulled my hand away. 'I said I'd do it when I get back.'

Jason was back to gripping the bench. 'Will you? Or are you just saying that so I'll give you the keys?'

I picked up the knife and finished splitting the pork belly. Then I washed my hands, dried them and held them out across the counter top for my keys.

'You missed a piece,' he said and I looked and saw the creamy white slice of pork fat stuck between my fingers. It looked opalescent, almost precious, not at all like the remains of a dead creature. I think Jason was struck by this too, because he stared at it for some time before dropping the keys into my palm beside that piece of dead flesh come to life. Then he left the room.

The cradle was never moved.

Jason went to work after that discussion and, instead of coming home to greet everybody, to pour drinks and to keep the conversation flowing, he sent me a text message five minutes before the guests arrived. *Baby needed a septostomy. Still in theatre. Be there soon. J.*

As I looked up from my mobile, my eyes caught a slant of pink light that fell from the setting sun onto the surface of Mémé's copper pots. I knew I had seen something like it before and my mind shifted through time, trying to reconcile image and memory. And then I knew.

A pink line on a white plastic stick.

My hands moved to my breasts, which I had thought, without really stopping to *think*, were fuller and more tender; it had been easier to ignore the tenderness because I'd assumed it was my milk ducts shutting down as they understood that their services were no longer required, that I was the kind of mother who couldn't even use the milk in her breasts. How was it possible that I could be a mother again? My intention had been something else entirely.

The first and only person I told was Imogen. She had let herself into the house and found me in the kitchen, transfixed by the line of light.

'Are you okay? she said. 'You look like you've seen a ghost.'

'I have.' I turned away from the shaft of sunset, towards Imogen. 'I'm pregnant again. It's too soon.'

Imogen touched her own just-pregnant belly, as though it were a charm. Then she hugged me. 'It'll be all right, Gaelle.'

Then the doorbell rang and I didn't even have to ask; Imogen stepped out to open the door and let the guests in. I stayed in the kitchen minding the cassoulet.

I heard four voices in the hall: Melanie, a former accountant, now stay-at-home mum to three boys; her husband Tony, a stockbroker for whom the word CrackBerry was invented as his every step was echoed by the electronic beep of incoming email; Gus, the only one of Jason's friends I could ever imagine sleeping with because he seemed as though he would never stray; and his wife Geraldine, a journalist (part-time, between children) who thought that beauty editors like me did nothing but attend lunches and launches and thread strands of adjectives together. Jason always said she was jealous but I thought she was snide.

'Hon, can you pour some wine,' I heard Imogen say to Alex, her husband. 'Gaelle's just finishing dinner.'

'We'll come and help,' Melanie replied. 'I haven't seen Gaelle for ages.'

I pulled my compact out of the bottom drawer and checked below my eyes for mascara pools but there were none, just clear tears, and so I blotted them away, hid the mirror and picked up two caipiroskas.

'Hi Gaelle.' Melanie swooped in for a kiss but I blocked her with the cocktail glass. 'Ooh, yum,' she said, taking a sip and turning to Geraldine. 'It's got mint in it.'

I handed Geraldine a glass.

'Cheers,' she said. 'You look great, Gaelle.'

'Not everyone keeps on an extra ten kilos after they've had a baby,' I said. I picked up my champagne glass and smiled. '*Salut.*'

If only you had said something about Aurora, I thought, then I wouldn't have been so rude. The last time I'd seen Geraldine I'd been heavily pregnant; surely an enquiry about the baby was required. It was as if I had not become a mother, as if even after having a baby, I still did not belong.

The silence was broken by the trotting sound of stilettos and Imogen stepping forward to say, 'That's got to be Rehana.'

And it was, the other friend of mine I'd invited, gorgeous Rehana, French also, like me; a cosmetics executive and the only single woman left in this world it seemed. She kissed both my cheeks and said, 'But you do look *magnifique, chérie.* I can never decide if it takes you hours to put yourself together or if you just fall out of bed looking perfectly groomed with all the right accessories.'

I laughed. 'Well if Jason was here you could ask him.'

'Still at the hospital?' Geraldine asked.

I didn't reply because Rehana was examining my cheekbones. 'That rouge is so light it looks like sunshine,' she said.

'It's your competition.' I pulled a silver case out of my bag and passed it to her. 'They sent me a load of stuff after Aurora was born ...'

'Look Gerry, cream blush,' Melanie squeaked. 'I haven't worn that since high school.'

Geraldine reached out a hand towards the compact at the same time as the cassoulet began to bubble so I said to Melanie, 'Keep it. I've got a dozen more in the bathroom cupboard.'

I walked between Melanie and Geraldine towards the stove and rolled my eyes at Imogen in the direction of the door. As I began to stir the pot I heard her say, 'Let's take our drinks outside and see what the guys are up to,' and I watched them file out, Melanie clutching her new blush, Geraldine empty-handed and Imogen and Rehana looking back towards me until the door closed behind them.

Jason was two hours late for dinner so I did not tell him about the new baby. He arrived with a box which he handed to me in the kitchen at the same time as he said, 'Ellie, I thought you would have eaten by now. But no one's had anything. Have you been out to say hello to anyone?'

'Dinner's not ready. Imogen's looking after everyone. I've spoken to the girls.'

'I bought this for you but it's too late for tonight; you're already dressed.' He gestured to the box.

I took off the lid and pulled out a dress. I frowned at the plunging neckline. 'This dress requires cleavage. I can't wear it. You'll have to take it back.'

'You haven't even tried it on. I just wanted you to know that I think you're beautiful.'

'I don't need a dress to tell me how I look.' I passed the box back to him.

'Sorry I'm late.'

I turned to the stove and tasted the cassoulet. 'It's ready.'

'I'll carry it.'

'I've got it.'

I was just about to push open the door when Jason said, 'I shouldn't have invited everyone.'

I could almost feel his flow chart terminate. He'd followed the *yes* arrow to this dinner party when he should have followed the *no*. I let the pot rest on a towel on my hip and turned back to look at my husband. We were standing in opposite corners of the kitchen, me cradling a pot whilst he had just picked up a bottle of wine and tucked it into the crook of his arm. I could hear Melanie laughing in the dining room and then Imogen's voice saying, 'She'll be out soon.'

'If we take this out,' I gestured to the food and the wine, 'then everybody can eat and then they'll leave.'

Jason's smile flicked on and I wanted to kiss his beautiful mouth. I felt as though we were almost back, as though perhaps we could get back to how we used to be. 'If we forget to serve wine they'll leave even quicker.'

'They know where the wine is. They'll just help themselves.'

He crossed the kitchen floor and brushed his hand across my ear lobe and around to the back of my neck. 'I'll get the door for you.'

And so we walked out to the dining room together. There were two empty chairs left, at opposite ends of the table.

'Jase,' Gus called. 'Empty glasses all round.' Jason stepped over to his friends and I could hear Gus continue. 'Haven't seen you in ages, mate. How're you doing?'

I put the pot down and it seemed as if the bang of the pot onto the wood fractured the women's conversation. I picked up a bowl and began to ladle cassoulet into it, then said, 'What did I interrupt?'

Everyone looked at Imogen. She sipped her drink and said, 'Gerry was just telling us about Felicity; she had her baby on the weekend.'

I picked up another bowl and filled it. 'What did she have?'

'A girl. Georgia.'

This time I looked at Geraldine; after all it was her story. 'Stitches? Vacuum? Epidural? I'm sure you've got all the details.'

Geraldine glanced at Melanie, then back to me. 'I don't know …'

I placed a bowl of food in front of Melanie. 'Really?'

Melanie put a forkful of cassoulet in her mouth and shook her head. It was Imogen who stepped into the role of spokesperson for the group. 'She had a natural birth. No stitches. No drugs.'

I laughed. 'Natural birth. With scented candles, I suppose. It's such a ridiculous phrase. There's nothing really that natural about having a baby in a hospital.' I could hear my voice becoming higher and louder so that Jason and then Gus and then everyone was looking at me. I plonked a bowl of food in front of Geraldine, another natural birth advocate who told me when I was pregnant with Aurora that all I had to do was drink raspberry leaf tea for the last eight weeks of the pregnancy and I would have a quick, easy birth. 'I've yet to meet anyone who can have an emergency caesar without drugs.'

'But no one gets a choice with an emergency caesar, Gaelle,' Geraldine said. 'Obviously that's not a natural birth.'

Silence spread across the table like an infection. Then Jason leapt up. 'Gus, pass your bowl over.'

I sat in my chair as Jason took the ladle from me and finished serving the dinner. He touched the back of my neck again as he passed but this time it was not like that tiny, shared moment of intimacy in the kitchen. I thought for a second about the baby I was supposed to be breastfeeding and the new baby inside me but reached for the champagne anyway and filled my glass. Then I frowned at Imogen and whispered beneath the clatter of cutlery, 'I've listened to all their labour stories. Why can't I talk about mine?'

'They're just afraid of all the stuff that no one likes to talk about.'

'But what if that's all you have?'

She did not answer because she could not.

THREE

I started back at work the following Monday, gladly exchanging shelves full of Johnson & Johnson Nursing Pads and Stayfree Extra Thick Maternity Pads for the thirty-two lipsticks sitting on my desk that were waiting to be described as sticks of creamy colour studded with diamond-shine. I tested the colours, which were just the wrong side of garish, and forced myself to remember that the readers of the magazine I worked for were: too young to be interested in investing in classic pieces; likely to wear a different shade of lipstick to work every day and wanting advice about how to successfully navigate their way through their twenties without ever stepping back into the youthful naivety from which they had just emerged, or crossing into the settled conservatism that they imagined lay in wait for them.

Imogen caught me studying the lipsticks when she came to check up on me. 'You look like you've forgotten what a lipstick is,' she said.

I lifted one up to show her. 'Don't you think they look like rattles, the way the base is shaped like a ball?'

She gave me that concerned look as if she too thought the same as everybody else, that two months after having a baby was too soon to be back at work.

So I laughed. 'I'm joking, Im. But wouldn't it be a great idea for the shoot? I'll dress the studio in white, get in a whole lot of naked babies and take shots of them playing with the lipsticks. Sort of avant-garde Anne Geddes.'

'I don't know, Gaelle. It'll be pretty hard to stage-manage babies. And if they're naked, you'll just end up with poop everywhere.'

'I know what babies are like, Imogen.'

An hour later I was in the staff kitchen making coffee and listening to people talking about bottle refusal, teething and waking after one sleep cycle. Opinions were sought about whether to resettle the baby, leave her to cry or get her up; mine was not. I recalled standing in the same kitchen, a year or so before, and half-hearing similar conversations above the bubbling of the coffee maker. I had nothing to offer such conversations then, but even now, after having Aurora, I was better suited to frothing the milk so it contained just the right amount of air than adding to the brew of advice surrounding me. My assistant turned around in the middle of her assertion that babies get windy when it's windy, saw me, and began to flap. 'Gaelle,' she looked at her watch, 'the meeting ... we're late ... sorry ... I'll get everyone to the boardroom now,' and flew out, trailed by a flock of sequinned and baubled editorial assistants.

So the conversation ended and the meeting began and minds turned to the magazine's annual Beauty Awards supplement and it was all going so well until I went that afternoon to the launch of a moisturiser with the expression-erasing properties of Botox. I stood in a bar that had been dressed in science-lab chic and drank white cocktails misted with dry ice while a boy—well, he was perhaps in his early twenties—gave us his marketing spiel, to which everyone pretended to listen while whispering conversations that went like this: Gaelle, you're back! You look great! Love your dress! Air-kiss, air-kiss. Darling, gorgeous, blah-blah ...

I replied with, 'It's so good to see you again,' or, 'So what are our freebies today? Handbags, jewels, spa weekends?' until I found Imogen and Rehana.

'I think all you get is a facial, chérie,' Rehana said as she kissed my cheeks. Then she nodded at the boy on the podium. 'He's new, he'll soon learn that Louis Vuitton handbags and a day at the Golden Door are required.'

'Still, it might be worth it if he's doing the facials,' I said.

Rehana laughed but Imogen frowned. And seeing the disapproval on her face, I felt for the first time the weight of the secret I carried in my womb and I made up my mind to tell Jason about the new baby. But then Janey from the new tweenie magazine, who'd been off on maternity leave herself, swooped into our group, smothered me with hugs and demanded, 'Gaelle, what did you have? I haven't heard anything about anyone while I've been away! I bet it was a girl. I bet she's gorgeous!'

I said, 'Yes, her name's Aurora,' and then listened for ten minutes while Janey described every detail of her baby's poo, sleep, puke and crying and could offer nothing but a stare in return when she asked me if I thought the amounts of each were normal. I remembered those conversations in the kitchen at work, at the dinner party, relentless conversations that followed me about like a shadow, and I knew that I couldn't tell Jason about the new baby and that, instead of telling Jason, I would take the boy on the podium with a pot of moisturiser in his hand to a room nearby with a view of the sea.

In my defence I can only put forward this disclaimer: I don't consider myself to be a promiscuous person. Promiscuity implies a degree of carelessness whereas I was very particular about who I slept with. The boy, for instance, I chose because he was vulnerable, as boys are. All I had to do was stand by his side at the bar, turn my body towards his and pout at my empty glass.

'I'm Mark (or Paul or Pete),' he said, taking the seat next to me.

'Hello,' I said and did not offer any more, not yet.

But that was all it took for him to begin to talk about himself, his job, the thing that he thought made him important. After a while he came to an end and then he said, 'What about you?'

Because he was new to the job and did not know who I was nor which magazine I worked for I said, 'I'm a photographer. Just starting out. It's the first launch I've covered.' That was the story I used because I knew it would appeal to his protective instinct—being small helped also; it made me seem more in need of protection when in fact the opposite was true. 'Your lashes were made to be photographed,' I continued and he blushed as I knew he would. It was true, though; his lashes were curved like Jason's hipbones and even at the time the comparison made me smile.

'You were made to be photographed, Gaelle,' he said and I laughed because it was the best he could do and he blushed again and insisted, 'You were.'

I waited until Imogen went to the ladies and then I took the boy's hand and led him away to a hotel near the harbour I'd discovered in these past two months; it was cheap enough that it didn't matter if I only spent an hour or so in the room but not so cheap that it didn't have linen on the bed with a five hundred thread count.

It was in those moments of time snatched in that neon-lit room by the water that I discovered that it was easier to escape with a stranger than with a husband, that the only way not to talk, not to think, was to do something else with my mouth, something else with my mind.

I thought very carefully about what I would do with the boy as we took the lift to the third floor, not speaking, surrounded by mirrors, but managing to avoid one another's eyes. The card beeped in the lock, the door clicked open and I led the way into the room and opened the curtains, wanting the room lit only by the lights drifting through the glass from life beyond. Then I laid the boy flat on his back across the bed and he let me because he was glad for once to have nothing to do, to have everything done for him. I took off his clothes but I did not take off mine; it excited him, the thought of what was hidden from view, and then I positioned myself over him, hovering, but did not take him inside even though he strained his arms towards me. He wanted to pull me down onto him but I moved away when he tried because I thought he should learn that he would get nothing he wanted if he did not do it my way. So I lingered on top, not quite touching him, until his penis began to jerk and only then did I slide down over him and let myself discover that the rhythmical movement of that boy's body beneath mine was all that I needed to make Aurora and Jason and the new baby disappear.

After he had wiped himself on the cotton bedsheets he lay down and closed his eyes, legs spread across the mattress, jaw relaxed, breathing beginning to slow.

'This isn't a sleepover,' I said and his eyes snapped open as if he'd almost forgotten why he was feeling so serene.

I held up my left hand and pointed to my wedding ring; it was a detail so fine but so weighty that I knew he would not have noticed it when he spoke to me at the bar. His scramble for clothes was almost comedic, in that slapstick, silent movie way, but I did not laugh because I had seen something through the window that caused me not to hear the click-bang as the boy left the room. Amidst the gilt-coloured dusk sitting over the water outside I saw another couple. She swam and he followed and I felt the gentle swell on the harbour flowing with ancient stories about women rising from the sea, spell-blinding men. Myths that explained nothing, like my wedding ring. It was a symbol of all that I was, all that I had to honour Jason. Then it became a curio, hiding a past long forgotten, buried bone-like beneath layers of dirty living.

FOUR

Imogen pounced on me the next day at work as I sat at my desk writing an article that extolled the virtues of the boy's miracle moisturiser.

'Have you told Jason yet?' she demanded.

'No.' I continued to type.

'When are you going to tell him? He'll be so excited to have another baby, Gaelle.'

'What if he's not?' I sighed as I looked up at her and then said, 'If he's home tonight, I'll talk to him about it.'

'I hope you do.' She paused and instead of leaving she shut the door to my office, sealing us inside.

I could feel, caught in the air, a moment of revelation.

The conversation that followed was full of silences and words that sat like clouds around our mouths. There was talk of an abortion scheduled for the day after tomorrow and a question, 'Will you come with me?'

To which the only response was, 'Yes.'

Then Imogen kissed my cheeks, as if thanking me. And I knew what she meant, what she would have said, if only such words existed.

Then it was the day before the abortion and we had to go to the launch of a new perfume.

'I don't know why I'm going to this,' Imogen said to me as we drove. 'Your readers will love it but mine will be just as happy to rub seawater on their wrists. It's all about the beach for fourteen year olds this summer. I've run out of words to describe bronze.'

'Bronzescent,' I supplied.

'Bronzine,' Imogen countered.

'Bronzoid.'

'Blah-onze.'

We both laughed.

'Besides, Rehana will never forgive us if we miss one of her launches,' I said. 'It'll be a good distraction. And she said the cocktails were fabulous. I need a drink. So do you.'

'You shouldn't drink.'

'French women drink all through their pregnancies.'

'You said that when you were pregnant with Aurora.'

The room we entered was full of music that beat at me like a memory. Quick–quick, strong–weak. The tango. Dancers strode the length of the floor, duelling with sensual precision. Tango. I hadn't known the perfume would be called that. I could not recall why the word bothered me so.

Imogen and I were sprayed with perfume by tanned and bare-chested men. The bouquet was woody, with a top note of iris. Lingering beneath, though, I smelled lilies. A fold of time past opened.

I sipped the drink in my hand and tried to follow Imogen but she was moving toward the blue lights on the dance floor so I stopped and let myself be scooped into a group of marketing executives who were all eager for the words in my beauty pages to speak favourably of their products.

We chatted, or rather they did, of sales figures and advertising campaigns. The tango of movement around us pressed closer. I tried to think of Jason and Aurora, but could feel such substantial things slipping away in the presence of all that was illusive.

Then, I don't know how—who manoeuvred it? Him? Or me?—I found myself talking to Lucas, Rehana's general manager, about cover mounts for the magazine, and all I could think was that he was nothing like Jason; he was olive-skinned but black-haired and had an aura of something about him that I recognised. Selfishness.

He wanted to lead me out to the dance floor but I couldn't do what I was about to do in public; that was a line I would not cross. So I told Lucas to meet me at the bar across the street. He bought me a drink, as I expected him to, and we sat on a sofa together, bodies close, as if we were intimate.

'You are very beautiful, Gaelle,' he said.

I laughed. 'You don't need to flatter me. I'm not going anywhere. Except here.'

I leaned in closer, placing my lips a kiss away from his. Then I stopped because I wanted him to be the one to take the final step. And he did, of course. He tasted different to

Jason, slightly bitter, and his kiss felt almost methodical.

I pulled away and watched him dangle in the space I had just occupied.

He adjusted his position quickly. 'Another drink?'

I laughed again. 'Is that the best you have to offer? I hadn't realised we were on a date.'

The only thing left to do after that was to go to a room with fine sheets where I tasted again those astringent lips and, even though my eyes were closed, I could see a woman—who was she?—as she undid Lucas's belt, opened the button on his trousers and pulled down the zipper, leaving his jacket, shirt and tie intact.

The woman found what she was looking for and her hand curled around it, holding on almost too tightly as she stroked, then she changed her grip so her fingers swept up and down, pulling harder with each movement. The man fumbled with her skirt, not quite, I'm sure, believing his luck, but it was too much for him and he had not the patience or self-control to wait until my skirt was pulled up and my knickers pulled down and I moved my body away just in time so the stain was on his clothes, not mine.

Then I went to the bathroom and closed the door. Washed my hands. Took enough time that he should have been gone by the time I emerged. But he wasn't. He was sitting on the end of the bed, trousers back on.

'What are you waiting for?' I asked.

He adjusted his tie. 'You. Your turn, Gaelle.'

I opened the door. 'I got what I wanted.'

He was silent a moment and then it was his turn to laugh. 'Whatever you say.'

After Lucas left, I sat on the unmade bed in the empty room, his scent stuck to the air, wondering what it was that felt missing, absent. There should have been something that came after the act: an epilogue, a coda, a closed bracket, like the stories my mother told me.

At half past eight the next day, I pulled up outside Imogen's house. She was waiting out the front, beneath a plane tree, and her beige coat blended so nearly into the trunk that she was almost disguised. She had her mobile phone in hand, dialling.

'My battery's dead,' I called out as I opened the car door.

She looked up with relief. 'I thought you weren't coming.'

'I wouldn't forget this.'

'No.'

As we drove, she stared straight ahead and said, 'I was thinking about the letters we used to write each other after you left London. About the things we thought were important back then. Make-up, magazines, boys.'

I tried to smile. 'You mean they're not important?'

But Imogen did not smile. 'Do you remember why we decided to come to Australia?'

I laughed. 'A holiday we forgot to return from.'

'No, the real reason.'

'Your mum died. You wanted to get away.'

'And you?'

I shrugged. 'Tired of goats cheese? We thought Sydney would be all sun, bikinis, beaches, tans. I never thought we'd both stay this long.'

'Me neither. I thought I'd go back to London after uni and get some high-powered job. I never thought you'd go back to France though.'

'No.'

'And now we've made our own families here, so we stay.'

I was unable to make my mouth move in reply. But Imogen barely paused.

'Remember the stories your mother used to tell us? Remem-ber how we thought, or maybe hoped—I don't know—that they were real?'

I nodded. 'I was thinking about that earlier. She thought they were real.'

'Yes, she did. But it didn't help her.'

'No.'

The reception area in that place for soon-to-be-dead babies was plastic-coated. Plastic chairs, laminated posters advocating contraception—although for anyone there it was a little too late for that—and the plastic faces of women who avoided looking at one another. Except Imogen and I. We sat side by side as I tried to fight the first trimester nausea that rose inside with every breath of air I took. We did not speak—speech seemed too frivolous—although I wondered if the baby would have liked to hear our voices for the last time.

Then it was time to let go of Imogen, to wait for her, to try not to think of what would happen.

'Take care.'

Which was, of course, something I should have taken well before then.

FIVE

As I walked up the path to my house I could hear, from somewhere, the crank of a speculum and the hiss of suction. Then I realised it was only the sound of branches tapping and leaves blowing.

On the street, I heard a mother call her daughter's name, loudly, several times, each call escalating in volume. It was the same as the way they called my name at the abortion clinic, over and over, louder and louder, because I sat still in my chair wondering why it was my name being shouted; they should have been calling Imogen's name. But eventually I stood and followed them into a room and changed into a gown.

There was one moment when I almost stopped, when I thought that perhaps Jason and I could do this again; we could become a mother and father to this baby too, rather than just a mother and father to Aurora. It happened as I sat on the bed and answered the nurse's questions; she was a muscular woman from too much time spent at the gym and I prepared to dislike her in the same way I disliked her lumpy body as I confirmed that I understood what I was doing and what the possible risks of the procedure were.

She came to my obstetric history and I readied myself for the counselling tone, the attempt to dissuade, but it did not come. The nurse's manner did not change, her eyes did not avert and her steadiness made me feel the absolute irreversibility, once again, of what was about to happen. But the only other option was to be pregnant again.

So I confirmed that I wanted conscious sedation. To feel relaxed and sleepy. Instead I felt not-there, as if I was in the reception area, still holding on tightly to the idea that it was happening to someone else, to Imogen, as if I was waiting for the body lying on the table, the body that was being opened up with a speculum and suctioned out. The body that was already so drained and listless and empty it was impossible to believe it could feel even more so.

And that was why, when Imogen dropped me home, I didn't go to bed and lie down as I should have done. Instead I stood outside the door to Aurora's room. I wanted to pick her up, to hold my daughter's trusting baby face next to mine, to imagine her with a brother or sister. I wanted to remember that she was something other than just an outcome of Jason and me. I knew that this was not why women ordinarily picked up babies and that this was also why Aurora could not help me. Because outcomes suggest endpoints, the thing that is left over, after. And there was nothing.

I walked outside and got into my car because I was tired of thinking about things I could not change.

The next day was my thirtieth birthday. Jason had organised a party for me on a boat in Sydney Harbour. I wore a dress which was the same colour as the water; it was one of the few things my mother had left behind and I was thinking about her as I stood at the prow listening to Jason step up behind me.

'Ready?' Jason asked as the boat began to move through the water. I nodded and took the glass of champagne from him. We chinked glasses and he said, 'Salut,' then, 'Happy Birthday.'

We looked at one another for a moment and I thought he might be about to kiss me but instead he said, 'I thought it'd be nice if we had half an hour alone before everyone came aboard.'

'Yes.' I moved my hands to the guardrail, watching the water split open so easily to let us through and I waited for him to say something supportive and encouraging, such as, It'll be fun, Ellie. You need a party. But he didn't. He stood beside me and held onto the guardrail too, looking into the distance, to where we were heading.

And even though I hadn't wanted words, I didn't want silence either. So my thoughts slipped out of my mouth and hit the water like glass on stone. 'We should have brought Aurora.'

Jason's eyes closed in on the point where the boat hit the sea. 'You know we couldn't, Ellie.'

'Why?' I did not mean why couldn't we bring her, I just meant: why?

Then Jason took hold of my arms and held me so tightly that I ached because he could never let go. His reply was so quiet and gentle that I could not take in his words because they were at odds with his tone.

I remember only the boat suddenly docking against a jetty lined with our friends; they were cheering and clapping and calling out, 'Happy Birthday!' As they boarded, Jason wanted to keep hold of my hand but too many people kept getting in the way and so we were left to manage without one another.

Before long, everyone was drinking Krug and we were floating past cliffs lit by constellations of houses. I was seduced into forgetting what Jason had said, seduced by the trouble to which he had gone to gather all my friends together, seduced by bubbles and still night air and the strand of pearls he looped around my neck. I let down my guard.

I saw Jason talking to Imogen, putting his hand on her slightly curved belly. He looked so sad that I stepped a little closer, wanting to know what he was saying.

'I want us to have another baby as soon as we can,' Jason said. 'But it's true what they say about sex after a baby, isn't it? There isn't any. Even for us.'

Imogen's surprise was of the kind that almost caused

her to spit the drink from her mouth. I knew then that all the lies had caught up with one another, as lies do, and that Imogen was stuck in the middle of both knowing and caring too much.

Jason took his hand away from her stomach and said, 'What?' half-jokingly, as if he expected her to laugh and tell him that the look on her face was nothing but a little belated morning sickness. She said nothing and so he asked again, 'What?' But this time the urgency in his voice said that he was not going to let her get away with evading the question.

So I did what I could to help.

I slotted myself into the space between Jason and Imogen and I finally let myself hear the words he had said earlier: Ellie, you can't keep pretending.

I was an expert in pretence. It was my inheritance. But I wanted to pass on so much more than just gaps and fantasies and lies. So I kissed Imogen's cheeks and this time she did not say, It'll be all right, Gaelle, but instead she left Jason and me to do what we had left to do.

'There was another baby,' I said.

It was not what Jason was expecting me to say. He shook his head, trying to understand. And I could see, written on his face, that he still wanted to forgive me, even then. 'But there couldn't have been ...'

So I let him look at my face because then I knew I wouldn't have to say it; I wouldn't have to tell him what I'd done.

His face became suddenly white. 'How could you? After

Aurora?' He was actually shouting. Something I'd never heard him do.

'You've answered your own question.' How could I? After Aurora.

'What?'

Neither of us moved for several seconds; it was as though we were posing, creating an image for an unseen camera. We were stilled and shaded, badly underexposed, all murky blacks and foggy blobs of rainbow colour. We had become the dead people pressed into a six-by-four rectangle of glossy paper and preserved beneath a sheet of framed glass, dead because we were no longer the people caught by the camera; we had left those creatures behind the second they were snapped. I was something else now. Some other kind of wife. Some other kind of mother.

I must have said this last sentence out loud because again Jason said, 'What?' as though the effort required to understand me was just too great. And that was why it was so easy to turn away from that Jason and from that Gaelle; the scene I was viewing belonged to them. I existed in the moments before the pose was assumed.

I felt the boat slow, then saw the jetty coming closer and heard only the softest splash of breaking water as I slipped over the side and swam towards the sand, reaching the shore before the boat docked, and then I ran towards the car and drove away, never looking back to see whether Jason was following me.

PART II

SIX

The trouble with running away wearing a party dress and carrying only a clutch full of make-up is that I am ill-equipped for my new life by the beach. At the very least, I need a bikini and something to eat. Fortunately, the service station at the end of the road sells both.

As I walk back to my cottage licking the oily salt from a hot-chip breakfast off my fingers, I can see that Siesta Park is a place of astonishing openness. A carpet of the softest moss-like lawn stretches down to scrub, which frames white sand and sea. The lawn is sprinkled capriciously with houses; they seem to have erupted like toadstools wherever it suited them. There are no fences. I do not know where the boundaries are, where my lawn ends and someone else's begins. The houses are an eclectic mix of weatherboard chalets left over from a deceased holiday park, and sleek interlopers straight out of the pages of a design magazine. My cottage looks like a nasty splinter stabbed into a mound of earth. It was all that was available.

I slip into my new bikini and sarong then leave the cottage, step across the lawn and follow the long lip of shore towards Dunsborough. The sea is breached by occasional jetties, their broken stumps worn smooth by the tides' fretting. Each jetty is covered with cormorants; at first they seem daubed into still life, wings outstretched, drying. But as I move closer they take off, tearing apart the illusion, leaving behind a blank canvas, gliding through air as if skating over ice.

Pieces of driftwood laze on the shore; I imagine they have travelled, like me, from somewhere exotic. One piece is semi-upright, arching forward, arms outstretched as if bewailing the dead. A pietà of wood.

After some time my progress is stopped by an estuary that breaks the shore in two, leaving me on one side, abandoned. It looks too deep, too brown, too squishy to cross so I walk into the ocean, topple and lie on my back in the water. Soft sea rolls over my belly, caressing it with liquid fingers. My ears fill with a sound like the hissing caught within seashells. The sound reminds me of Jason's voice, demanding, How could you? After Aurora? But of course After Aurora is why I am Here on the other side of Australia, why Jason is There, back in our home in Sydney, and why Aurora is Somewhere Else.

Most days I wake too early to an expanse of unfilled hours. Every morning there is a circle of blood on my white cotton underwear and I think about the doctor's words: come back for a check-up in four weeks. I throw the underwear in the bin and contemplate not going into the water but I suppose it will make no difference now so I swim, regardless.

My phone rings occasionally but I do not answer it. I check the messages, though. There is never one from Jason. There are several from Imogen.

'Where are you?'

'I just want to know if you're okay.'

'Jason is beside himself.'

There's a message from a man whose voice I do not recognise. 'Gaelle, we should … ahhh … catch up again. Soon. Umm … call me. If you want to.'

And then my favourite message. From Margaret, my mother-in-law. 'Gaelle, running away is not a luxury you can afford.'

I almost text back to her: Nor was staying.

One last message, from Mémé and Pépé. 'Gaelle, please call.'

But I can't. Even though my grandparents are the only ones who will not require an explanation, their understanding is more than I can bear.

Every morning I walk to the estuary, swim, turn around, walk back. My twin-lens reflex camera is my only companion, besides the rays surfing the shallows, keeping just ahead of my brisk shadow. I wonder at the luck of leaving the camera in the car, of forgetting to take it onto the boat, of at last having time to spend with this old friend. I sit on the beach, photographing the transition from dark to dawn to day, feeling the minutiae of elapsed time and wanting to wrap myself within this span of unconscious day. It is the same feeling I had not quite three months ago as I sat photographing a different dawn the day after Aurora was born. Jason had passed me a package of photos that he'd taken of Aurora the day before and I only had to look at them briefly to see that they were as mundane as I had expected them to be. Photos of newborn babies all tend to look the same and these were no different: a plastic doll left out in the sun too long, skin shrivelled, flesh purple from knowing only womb-shrouded darkness.

I wanted something more spectacular for Aurora's first photographs. So that was why, when Jason left, I eased myself out of bed, careful not to split a stitch, and picked up my camera. I took shot after shot of the dawn light laid over the sky and its becalmed reflection in the harbour. Then I slipped down to the hospital pharmacy with my roll of film and waited for one hour.

When I returned to my room I tucked the pictures of the two halves of the dawn light into Aurora's crib so they would be the first thing she saw when she woke. I sat on the bed and watched her, knowing that at last I had a photograph that shouted, as a photograph should, look at me!

'Here for a holiday?'

My vision of Aurora is replaced by rubber thongs cutting into ankles layered with coils of flesh. I don't look up at the person in front of me. 'No.'

'Work?'

'No.'

'Family?'

I laugh and cannot stop. I can hear myself cackling like a hysteric and the woman hurries away, scared of my apparent madness. There is absolutely no reason why I am here. The last flight out of the airport on the night of the party was going to Perth; I lived in Perth for a couple of years when I was young, with my mother. A feature in an airline magazine showed me a place called Siesta Park, nestled in a bay that curved like a cupped palm, midway between Busselton and Dunsborough. Warm. Protected. Safe. And unfamiliar; a place with no reminders. I hired a car. I drove. Here I am.

I laugh until I am exhausted from gasping and until I realise that, in the sound of sucked air, I can hear my childhood or, more precisely, my mother.

I stand up, shake off the past and wonder where the woman came from. When I reach the lawn leading up to my cottage, I see. People have arrived at the other houses. They are gathered in a circle of plastic chairs, chatting, laughing. Their children are spread across the lawn, marking the territory as unclaimable, Any-Man's Land. I walk past, head down so as not to be disturbed, but the people call out, 'Hello!'

I wave without looking up, then slide into my house.

Now I am trapped inside. I want today and tomorrow to be like yesterday: still mornings of steamed grass, the afternoon snapping with cicada clicks and the evening simmering with the white-sharp scent of peppermint trees. Later, I peep outside and see the people, still in a circle, still laughing, still chatting. They have lit a bonfire and everybody seems to come and go from the surrounding houses to this warm space with an ebb and flow that is as natural as the tide. There is no need for introductions or formalities. They blend, shift and absorb, like children.

I go to bed and listen to the long forgotten sounds of night away from a city: shifting earth, the movement of air, water breathing. Rural lullabies, which send me into a dream-filled sleep.

In my dream, Jason is sitting on the edge of our bed at home, surrounded by white sheets that seem to crack like ice around him. His head is gripped in his two hands, his body shivers and the sound he makes is primitive. In anyone else I would say it was an expression of grief, but I have never seen his feelings so exposed. I walk up behind him and watch for a while, wondering who the grief is for—me? Himself? Aurora? Or perhaps it is hope? No, not hope. It had always been me who mourned hope. Never Jason.

The sound of thumping on the roof wrenches me back into my skin. I get out of bed, pick up my camera and go to the window. I photograph over and over the women and children in plastic chairs around the bonfire. A girl whose red hair has just been twined into a braid gets up and spins in a circle, smiling at her mother. I steal that moment then put the camera away. The thump on the roof continues. Possums.

The next day I set out early on the cobwebbed bike that I found in the shed, determined to escape the neighbours. I cycle along a path that is lined on one side by sea so flat it is possible to discern the precise place where the water changes from chartreuse to cobalt to the colour of Jason's eyes. On the other side of the path, caravan parks, borderless, blend in a stretch of summer holiday joy all the way from Dunsborough to Busselton. I dodge children so enticed by limitless ocean that they forget to look where they are going, dogs gone mad in the morning sun and couples so enraptured in themselves and ice-cream that they do not realise the ringing of a bell is not, in fact, Cupid's song, but a woman on a bike who does not care for dogs or children or lovers.

I turn off the path near The Goose Café and weave through pedestrian snarls until I reach the town centre. When I see a Kodak sign in a shop window, I stop, go inside and join a queue of sweaty people who are collecting their photos.

I stare around the room at the plastic ferns grey with dust, once colourful posters faded by sun, and printers expelling photograph after photograph, pages of captured visions.

I ignore the self-serve kiosks, hold onto my canister and say to the red-haired woman behind the counter, 'Matt paper, singles, and don't adjust the colour balance, thanks.'

She glances up from her pen. 'Anything else?'

'I'd like them in an hour.'

'Fine.' She holds out the docket. I take it and drop the canister into her palm then leave.

I cycle down to the beach to sit and wait but the air is full of squeals and laughter and coconut oil. The café beckons, or rather the smell of coffee does, but the fish and chippy perkiness of the place is too much.

I return to the photo shop and sit on a chair. *Woman's Day*'s 'Make-up Tip of the Month' beckons to me from beneath the face of a celebrity whose name I can't be bothered remembering. I put the magazine down.

'I like this one best,' a voice announces.

A girl of about thirteen stands in front of me, holding one of my photographs. Her relationship to the woman at the counter is indicated by the same set of red curls pulled back into a ponytail.

'Glenda,' the girl points to a shop assistant, 'wanted to know why you'd taken a photo of the beach and chopped off the water. She said you needed to frame your pictures better.'

'It's not a photo of the beach. It's the dawn light.' I put out my hand for the photograph.

The girl ignores my hand. 'I told her it was a photo of the sun hiding behind the sky.'

A child's eyes. Instruments of perfect seeing. The girl and I stare at one another. I turn away before she sees too much.

'Selena!' The girl's mother leaves the queue of holiday-snappers to Glenda and takes my photograph from her daughter. 'Sorry,' she says. 'My daughter helps out during the holidays for pocket money. I don't let just anyone wander round the shop with my customers' photos.'

She finds the rest of my order, puts the photograph in the packet and passes it to me. 'These are good.'

'I know.'

I hand the woman some money and walk away. As I push open the door, I look back at the girl. She shakes her head at me.

SEVEN

There is no escape from the rapping on the door. I peek through the curtains and see a group of women: Siesta Park's uncontained neighbours. I feel conned. Nowhere in the airline magazine had it said that Siesta Park had an attitude of we're all in this together. It must be a pose; surely beneath the idyllic holiday pastoral, something more authentic must lie.

I press on a half smile, not too much, and open the door.

'You can't just sit in here by yourself,' one of the neighbours says. 'We're all friends; we don't wait for invitations. I'm Julie.' She pushes her hand through my half-open doorway.

I shake it briefly and say, 'I'm Gaelle. Visiting from Sydney.'

I watch them swirl my name around their mouths, unsure. It is not Gale. Or Gayle. But something longer. Musical. Foreign.

Julie breaks into the silence. 'I love Sydney shopping. Must be a bit dull for you here.'

'I used to live in Perth when I was young.'

'Come and join us later for tea. We'll get out the cheese

and a few bottles of our famous Margaret River red.'

'Lovely,' I say. I will stay for half an hour. Long enough not to be rude but short enough not to be friendly.

I walk over to the circle of women sitting in green plastic chairs to which they seem permanently adhered. Most of them are mothers; I can tell because their faces have been marked by their children in the same way that mine is now marked. They appear to have no cares. Actually, I am wrong; they care about relaxing, having a holiday, enjoying themselves. I can tell by the noise; it is uninhibited.

I stand apart, in the shadows of the fire, eye suddenly caught by a flash of red. The mother and daughter from the photo shop.

'Hi Gaelle,' the girl shouts.

I wonder two things; how does she know my name and how is it that she can pronounce it properly?

The girl's mother approaches. 'Hi, I'm Marie. And this is Selena. Julie's my sister-in-law.'

We shake hands and I nod at the girl.

'Been taking any more photos?' Marie asks.

'No. I haven't seen anything worth photographing.'

The girl leaps into the foreground of our conversation. Wisps of her hair flash in the firelight, transformed to filigree. Or a crown, albeit of the devilish kind. 'You can photograph me,' she says.

'I don't photograph people.'

'Why not?'

I look to her mother, expecting her to admonish the girl for being so pushy. But her mother is suddenly busy with cheese and wine and chatter. The girl does not back down into the silence. Instead, her stare and her eyes dare me to answer.

'Because a photograph traps you in the past.'

'Show me.'

I shake my head, ready to refuse; I have nothing to prove to a thirteen year old girl, but there is something about the way she looks at me that makes me say, 'All right Selena, I'll take your photograph.'

'Yes!' The girl's mouth skips into a smile.

The corners of my mouth turn up also; she is infectious, although in the manner of a disease.

'I have to get my camera,' I say.

'Make sure you come back,' she says and I want to slap her for being so prescient.

When I return, she is standing with her mother. 'They're having an exhibition at the town hall in a few weeks,' Marie says. 'They want amateur photographers to send in pictures they've taken down here over summer. You should send in your stuff.'

Before I can demur, Selena interrupts. 'Where do you want to do it? I could swing in the tree. Or jump on the trampoline.'

'The tree'd be great,' Marie says.

'I think the trampoline would be better,' I say, walking away.

Selena bounds onto the trampoline and begins to bounce, arms flying up and down like wings in time to the rise and fall of her body. Against the black sky, the light of my flash recovers her image and connects her to whoever will later view these pictures. Pictures of a blurred girl in flight with filigree hair etched into the night.

I am having a cup of coffee the next afternoon when the screen door opens and Selena enters. She flops into the sofa. 'Do you like this colour?' she asks, propping her feet on the coffee table and flexing her toes. 'Mum reckons it's tarty. But she never paints her nails.'

I examine the dark burgundy polish, get up and take a coral bottle from a colourful row on the kitchen bench. 'This is more summery. Bring it back when you've finished with it.'

'Cool!' She grins and tucks the bottle in her pocket. Then she looks around my cottage and says, 'You don't have much stuff, do you?'

I see the cottage through her eyes for a moment: black sarong and bikini perched like crows on the chair outside, a kitchen bench scattered with jars of coffee, nail polish, sunscreen and moisturiser, white thongs waiting beside the door and camera and photographs pushed to one side of the dining table. There is even less in the bedroom but the door is closed and she cannot see that. I shrug. 'I travel light.'

'You look like the kind of person who'd have loads and loads of matching luggage.'

I shake my head. 'I never take more than I can carry.'

Selena yawns and stretches and something in her pocket crackles. She stands and says, 'Mum said to give you this.' She hands me a flyer for an exhibition.

I put it in the bin while Selena picks up a roll of film from the table. 'Are these the ones of me?'

I nod.

'When are you going to get them developed? I want to see what they're like.' She starts to twirl, posing I'm sure, wanting to be fixed again in silver halides, painted into the light.

'I don't like other people developing my photos.'

'But you went to our shop the other day.'

'I didn't have much choice.'

'And if you hadn't, then you'd never have met me.' She stops twirling and grins.

A laugh escapes from my mouth. 'That would have been terrible.'

Selena moves towards the door. 'I know a darkroom you could use.'

I say nothing, but wait, because I can see the words are about to spill off her tongue regardless of whether or not I show any curiosity.

'Mum's set one up for me at the shop. It's kind of in the

cupboard with the cleaning stuff but it works fine. You could use it if you want. Then you'd have to show me the photos.' She fixes her eyes on me, daring me again.

The faces we pass as we cycle are, at this time of the day, sun-weary and slightly glazed. Feet trudge rather than run, bodies itch with stuck-on sand and parents wheedle exhausted children to walk just a few more steps. Selena and I weave past carelessly; she pedals almost too fast, looking over her shoulder every now and again, expecting me to keep up. I do, just.

We arrive at the shop half an hour later. Selena pushes open the door and calls, 'Mum, Gaelle's going to use my darkroom. She said she'd help me with some of my photos.'

Marie looks up from the queue of people and says, 'Thanks for helping Selena. I don't get much of a chance over the summer with the shop so busy.'

Her graciousness almost makes me ashamed and I find myself saying, 'I'll make a copy of the photos of Selena for you.'

'Thanks.'

'C'mon Gaelle,' Selena tugs my hand. 'It's over here.'

She opens the door to a walk-in cupboard lined on each side with a bench. There is a sink in one corner, and mops, brooms and buckets in another.

'Ignore that stuff,' she says, following my gaze. 'See, I've set it up properly, there's a wet side and a dry side and all my trays are in the right order—develop, stop, fix—and when you shut the door it's really dark.' Her hand jumps from item to item and when she finishes she looks at me expectantly.

'It's great.'

She grins. 'I think so. You can use it first if you want. Then I'm going to develop the film from my dive at the jetty last week.'

'My husband dives. He likes the silence beneath the sea.' I picture Jason for a moment, wetsuited, swimming with fish, and Aurora, when she is about six, floating alongside, chasing seahorses. I turn away from Selena and pick up a film reel, but it doesn't matter; she doesn't ask the question I am expecting: *why isn't he here?*

She just says, 'Yeah, it's pretty quiet down there.'

And then it is quiet in the darkroom and I begin to transfer the girl from film to negative to paper. What emerges is what I want; I have split two exposures over a single negative. The first image of the girl leaping off the trampoline is spread over an earlier image of the dawn light. Selena is overlaid on the sky, in smeared motion, arms extended. A haloed shadow accompanies her body; it looks like the soul, exposed. And now that the image is fixed, I am unable to separate what appears accidental from what was intentional. Which is as it should be.

'Can I see?' Selena peers over my shoulder.

I slide the prints beneath blank paper. 'They didn't work.'

'Oh.' The girl is, for once, lost for words but she recovers quickly. 'Can you help me with mine? I want them to look like it really is down there under the sea. Like another world.'

Then my hands are busy with practical matters, showing her how to develop her images so that behind the fish darting through coral there is a girl, suspended, floating in water. The girl's eyes command the viewer to look at her, not the fish.

Selena shrieks when the image emerges. 'Excellent! That's exactly what I wanted.' Then her face falls. 'I'm not sure Mum'll like them though.'

'Mothers are used to being disappointed.'

It is evening when we cycle back. The path is ours alone, everybody else is barbecuing; the smell of fried onion and burnt sausage stalks us all the way to Siesta Park. In the almost-light, the scrub and the sand dunes seem wilder and less bucolic than they did earlier; it is almost as if we are riding through the underside of this holiday paradise.

Selena stops just before we reach her house and turns to me, cheeks flushed, eyes bright against the dusk.

'Take a photo of me now, Gaelle,' she says, and takes off again, riding around in a circle, arms lifted off the handlebars, grinning.

And even though it's a pose of the worst kind, I pull the

camera out of my backpack, move closer to her and use the difference between what I see in the viewing lens and what the film will see in the taking lens to misalign her head and shoulders. I want the error. The detachment. The vanished body.

After the flash fades, Selena turns her bike towards home. Then she stops. 'Do you have kids, Gaelle?'

'Yes. One. She's just a baby.'

'I thought you did.' She cycles away, waving.

'Why?' I start to ask, but stop. She moves too quickly on her bike; she cannot hear me now. The words come out anyway, in a whisper. 'Why did you think that?' She could tell that I was a mother. Why is she the only one who can?

EIGHT

I am returning from the beach to my cottage, which I have learned to leave unlocked because burglars are as common in Siesta Park as reticent neighbours. But the door is open. Someone is inside. A long-suppressed bubble of hope rises in my throat. Jason. Aurora. They've come to find me.

My feet race along with my heart and I almost pull the screen door off its hinges.

'Jason.' I stop.

Selena is standing next to the table, beside the photographs I developed with her the other day. She is holding her folded towel against her chest. The pile of pictures is no longer tidy.

I lean against the doorway. 'Find what you were looking for?'

She shakes her head too vigorously. 'I was just waiting for you. I only looked at the ones on top.' Her face is flushed with lying.

I'm curious to know what she's up to but the way to find out is not to ask. She'll slip up. People always do.

'Hey, let's walk to Dunsborough,' she says, joining me at the door, suddenly eager to leave. 'Have you been there yet?'

'No. Everyone says it's too touristy.'

'Well Busso's better. But you can't come all the way here and not see Dunsborough. All the cute surfers hang out there.'

'Any particular cute surfer you want to see?'

Selena blushes. 'Nah. They only want city girls. They'd think you were hot.'

'A little old, perhaps.'

She shrugs. 'Half of them probably don't care about stuff like that.'

'How far is it?' Far enough, I hope, for her tongue to loosen about her search through my photos.

'Dunno. Maybe an hour. It'll be fun.'

'But we have to cross the estuary.'

'It's low enough to walk through in the morning.'

'What if the water is higher on the way back?'

'It never gets higher than my head.'

We don't speak until we reach the estuary which, as Selena had promised, is no deeper than ankle height. But there is the matter of the sand below the water. It looks like the surface of the moon. Soft. Spongy. Craterous with indentations like egg cartons. And it is the brown colour of sewage from the iron and nutrients passing into the water upstream. I place one toe in and immediately withdraw it. The sand feels as it looks.

Selena is already halfway across. She turns to look back at me and stands, hands on hips, shaking her head.

I creep my foot forward and am ready to pull it away as quickly as I had withdrawn my toe but Selena takes my action for acquiescence. She is in front of me, grabbing my hand and I have no choice but to follow or fall. She runs, splashing, through the water and so do I. Her laughter fills the air with a lightness that lifts the sun and the gulls and the breeze to flight. By the time we reach the other side I am laughing too.

'See, told you it'd be fun,' she says.

'Yes. You did.'

We begin to walk again, past a family loading a speedboat with picnic hampers to take to their yacht which is moored further out; it sits on top of the water like a grounded cloud.

Selena says, 'Do you think they're running away?'

'Why would they be running away?'

'Maybe the lady's in disguise and she isn't really who she says she is. Someone might be on her tail and she has to escape before anyone discovers her true identity.'

I shade my eyes and watch the speedboat leap like a dolphin over the waves. 'Yes. Her identity is something she would want to protect.'

'Now it's your turn.' The girl looks at me.

It seems we are playing a game.

I look around. There are two stingrays in the water. They have been following us for a while, darting in to the shore every now and again to peer at us through gentle eyes. They will have to do.

'The stingrays are really our guardians,' I say. 'Their tails are wands which pass magic through their electric charge. If we were brave enough to be stung, we would have everything we ever wanted.'

Selena grins. 'I knew you'd be good at this.'

'Yes, make-believe is my forte. I was taught by a master.'

'Who?'

'My mother.'

Selena flops down on the sand, stretches and closes her eyes. 'What was she like?'

I look back to the other side of the estuary, to the spot where I sit every day, alone. I look at the girl lying on the sand next to me. At her age, I would have been one of the girls chasing after the surfer boys in Dunsborough. I would never have befriended a thirty year old woman who continually met enthusiasm with detachment. But, other than detachment, nail polish and photography are all I have to offer. I doubt that they will last the summer. Selena's game has made me think of something else I can contribute. I can tell her the story of my mother. Given it is a story that has no end, it should last us till the weather cools.

PART III

NINE

I was six years old when my mother came to collect me from my grandparents' farm in France as if I were simply a piece of luggage that had been misdirected. I had never expected to be granted a mother-creature and only knew of their existence because the children on the neighbouring farms all had one and because I had heard about them in fairytales: mothers died tragic deaths so their children could be persecuted by evil stepmothers, or they made promises to give their children away in return for magic powers. Knowing this should have made me more careful.

Selena's voice breaks in, expressing disbelief already. 'You didn't see your mum till you were six?'

I shake my head. 'I don't remember her before then. I'm sure she must have been there initially, when I was a baby. But not after that.'

'Wow.'

'If I interrupted my mother when she was telling me a story, she'd stop telling it.'

'I'm glad your mum's not telling the story then,' Selena grins.

'Shall I keep going?'

She nods.

◞

On the morning my mother was to arrive I woke early and went downstairs to the kitchen where Pépé was sitting at the table with a bowl of *café* and a hunk of bread and pâté.

Mémé smiled at me as I walked into the kitchen, her face rippling with lines like a puddle. 'Why are you up so early, *chérie*?'

'Because Maman is coming today.'

Pépé gulped the rest of his *café*, stood and left the room, leaving behind a trail of breadcrumbs. I moved to follow him, to demand my morning kiss, but Mémé propelled me into a chair.

'Pépé is busy today. Have your breakfast.'

That accomplished, I set off along the track cut through the long grass by Pépé's van to wait at the gate for the arrival. I watched, for what I thought was a long time, the dirt road that linked our farm to civilisation but the dust remained still, unstirred by car tyres. I closed my eyes and listened for unfamiliar sounds amidst the goats' bleating. Nothing.

As the sun rose, my legs began to tire and my skin to sweat. Dust stuck to my face. I itched. I was sure it was lunchtime but I knew that if I turned away, then she would arrive and I would miss the spectacle.

'Gaelle!' Mémé was approaching. 'Time for your nap.'

I shook my head and clung to the gate. But Mémé's arms, made strong by years of herding goats, prised my fingers away, lifted me up and took me home to bed.

I woke to an unfamiliar sound, like pebbles shifting on a shore. I listened for a minute, realised the sound was laughter and followed it out to the kitchen.

A crowd of aunts, cousins and uncles from the neighbouring farms was gathered around the long oak table. Rows of copper pots flashed into the room like miniature suns and my nostrils filled with the fresh, charred scent of Pépé's goats cheese. A stranger was seated at the head of the table and I watched her as she spoke.

'I wore false eyelashes, and ostrich feathers in my hair, and every night I danced the cancan in the biggest casino of all where the hotel rooms had round beds raised on plinths, satin sheets and mirrored ceilings. Vegas is like Paris surrounded by desert. Full of light.'

Selena laughs. I frown. 'Sorry Gaelle,' she says, 'but I've never heard anyone's mum talk like that. If my mum found a set of false eyelashes she'd probably think they were caterpillar legs. And there's no way she'd ever dance the cancan, whatever that is.'

'You should ask her. Sometimes mothers surprise us.'

Selena considers this. During the pause, I stare at a child on the jetty, throwing a handline into the water, leaning out almost too far, pulling back just in time. Other than me, Selena and the fishing child, there is nobody else on the beach. If the child were to fall in, would we get there in time, I wonder. There is no current to take the child anywhere; its body would seesaw with the water's breath, thumping into a pylon with every exhalation. I turn back to Selena.

She is watching the child too, watching the reeling in of the handline, the disappointment of no catch, the recasting of the line back into the water. 'Maybe.'

꒰

When I was six, I had never heard anyone talk like my mother either. I remember turning my attention to my aunts and uncles, expecting a boisterous outburst of mockery. But there was only the bubbling sound of expectation. They were spellbound. Was it because of the tale she was telling or the way she looked? Both were equally unexpected. Feathers and false eyelashes were as common in our village as the blue satin shorts, brief as underpants, which this woman wore.

Now, looking back, I wonder if my relatives were not actually captivated. Perhaps they were simply afraid to interact with someone who'd become known as the black sheep, scared that her blackness would contaminate them with its exuberance, its absence of limitation. Or they could have been suppressing floods of scorn at her inappropriateness; what use, after all, are oriental embroidered clogs when one has to traipse all day through dust and *caca*.

I must have made a sound and betrayed my spying because Mémé held out her hand to me. 'Gaelle! You're awake. Here's the person you've been waiting all day to see.'

She patted me in the direction of the barely dressed sorceress, who opened her arms. I was transfixed by her fingernails, which were long and gold and therefore made for casting spells. I stood back and waited, assessed. Perhaps that was my mistake. If I'd run straight into her arms like a good daughter should, then everything would have been all right. The mother–daughter bond would have conquered all.

Before I had decided what to do, Pépé stood and said, 'Gaelle needs to come with me. Check the goats. There might be a storm.'

He picked me up before my mother could reply and carried me out to the hall. He stopped only to get our boots and to put me down and then he began to march away, towards the forest, so fast that I had to run like the dogs at his heels to keep up. Pépé slowed to lift me over the wire fence and only began to walk at my pace once we were tucked away into the trees.

The forest was bedded down, ready for slumber. The silence hurt my ears after the fullness of sound in the room we had just left so I said to Pépé, 'Why is Maman here?'

He bent down, picked up a rock and passed it to me. 'Gaelle, what colour is this rock?'

'Grey. But why ...'

'Or is it blue?'

I laughed and was about to say no, but I stopped. The top side of the rock, coloured by light tipping through leaves, did have a bluish hue.

'What colour do you think the rock will be if we come to find it tomorrow morning?' Pépé continued.

I thought for a moment. Mornings were usually muddy, the colour of truffles. Perhaps the rock would be too. I was about to say so but he did not wait for my answer. 'Things always change, Gaelle. Even here. Some changes suit us, some don't.' He dropped the rock and then said something I'd heard him say so many times before, usually after too many bottles of vouvray. 'I'm an accidental farmer, Gaelle. I was going to catch the train to Calais and then a ship to New York. See the Empire State Building. But responsibility caught me first.'

I used to wonder what this responsibility was, what it meant. Now I know. A farming legacy left by his parents. A dead older brother. Also me. And Maman.

❧

This time I am the one who interrupts the story, not with words but with silence. Selena doesn't say anything for once; she waits on the sand, eyes closed, trusting that I will continue when I am ready.

The child we were watching earlier is still standing on

the jetty, fishing, catching nothing. But the casting and reeling in and checking continue, over and over. The look of expectation remains on the child's face; the trickery of hooked seaweed does not diminish it. Selena's face, shiny with sunscreen, bears the same look. It is an expression of childhood and I wonder when adulthood will begin to encroach on her forehead, slowly erasing all traces of wonder. Watching them both, I know that Selena and the child will have no need to tell stories about their past when they are older because they have not given their childhoods away.

I turn away from the child, back to Selena and continue.

∼

My six year old self dreamt that night about being locked in a land inhabited only by my mother. The land shifted and moved and nothing there was familiar except the repetitive sound of an unknown voice, like a nursery rhyme.

I woke up with the shifting feeling inside my stomach; it made me catalogue my room as if it too would soon shift away.

There was the torn but still beautiful silk-covered dressing screen that Mémé said had protected the modesty of young women for hundreds of years. Mémé also said it was the one remaining treasure of our house's former glory. The screen was embroidered with castles and peacocks and *tournesols*—sunflowers—with their heads lifted up to the sky. And the walls of my room were heavy, pungent with bouquets of peeling wallpaper.

As I remember this, I want to laugh because now, of course, such things are fashionable and dozens of shops in Woollahra sell imitations of the furniture and accoutrements of my childhood. Back then, our version of French shabby chic was merely shabby and not at all chic. How artificial the items in those shops now seem, the artifice intensified by the rooms in Sydney to which they are transferred—there is too much openness. The genuine articles are meant for rooms caught and bound and walled; the space of an open plan has a temporary feel at odds with timelessness.

Then I began to hear real voices, loud voices, voices caught and bound in the rooms downstairs, so I slid down the stairs and sat on the floor behind the closed kitchen door.

'I have a wonderful new job without so much night work. And good money. I can look after Gaelle.' It was my mother's voice.

'What is this wonderful new job, Lili?' It took me a moment to work out that this was Pépé's voice. There was a tone to it that I had never heard before.

'I don't have to explain everything to you. My word should be enough.'

'Your word! The word of a mother who abandons her child is worth nothing.'

'I want to get to know my daughter.'

'If you take her now, she's yours. We don't want you back.'

My mother's voice snapped like broken bone. 'I won't ever be back.'

She marched out so quickly that I didn't have time to slip back to my room. She saw me there, laughed and squatted down to tuck a piece of hair behind my ear. 'Gaelle, we are the same, you and me.'

At the time, I did not understand it was a wish rather than a prophecy.

The next day I offered to take her on a tour of the house and land. It didn't occur to me that she used to live there; people who looked like Maman did not grow up on farms.

Our farm was in the Loir-et-Cher *département* of the Vallée de la Loire and my grandparents were in the less than glamorous business of goats cheese. They were one of several local producers who prided themselves on their traditional method of manufacture. No selling out to a dairy for them. They were protecting a heritage, preserving an idea, commemorating a past with the sort of love and attention it probably didn't deserve—what had it done for any of us, this past?

No, the past had simply absconded and left behind a few farmhouses which gathered together in pretence of a village, although we were lacking even the necessary church to grant us such status. We barely even had a road, just a potholed track that blew in more dust than visitors. Once upon a time—so Pépé would tell me—the aristocracy lived there at the edge of the forest but they had migrated with the kings to Amboise and Chenonceau centuries ago, abandoning their petits chateaux, which were promptly demoted to the position of farmhouse or wine cellar. Remnants of grandeur lingered in the sun-faded tapestries and carved wooden ceilings but, year after year, roofs sagged further beneath the weight of an uncertain future and buildings leaned exhausted against the air.

I only understood this later, of course, when I returned to the farm as a teenager and spent a few years there before I came back to Australia to go to university. As a child I saw little more than cuddly goats and grandparents, fresh cheese for breakfast and the space to run and run and run, a collage of pastoral moments interrupted by my mother.

I can see us now as we traipse from stone room to stone room, our similarities. Her eyes the colour of almost-night. Char-edged gold. Our smallness, a thinness that would always reveal our stress and worry, hers marked but invisible to me then. And our foreignness, a quality that never failed to betray us, not just in accent, gesture or physical features, but in carriage, word choice and demeanour, a coolness that clung to our skin and set like ice around our hearts. Learned traits. I learned them from her. From whom did she learn them?

'Our house used to be a petit château,' I said to my mother as we walked.

'Really?' she said, feigning surprise with such authenticity I did not realise it smacked of the highly practised art of a liar.

'But then the *Comte* moved away and the château was ruined because no one lived here. Except ghosts,' I embellished, anxious that I not lose her attention.

'Ghosts? Yes, this house is full of ghosts,' my mother said as she stared at the fading paintings hanging on the walls of the hall—paintings that I could reproduce now, almost exactly, because I bore their stares most of my teenage years. They were Dutch and French treasures left behind by the original owners and thus clearly of little value, but which had since been bequeathed by my family through generations. The paintings were religious, immune to colour, heavy with brown and black and grey—a pietà, the *Judgement of Solomon*, a nativity.

'Some things really do not change,' she said as she turned away.

I showed her outside, to where Mémé was in the kitchen garden, digging scraps into the dirt. I pointed out some of my favourite things: the gravel path embraced by the unpruned arms of lime trees, a feast of aromatic herbs, and the empty riverbed, calligraphied with rivulets of nearly evaporated water. My mother glanced at each sight and said yes as if affirming its presence but unable to do more. Then we stepped across to the dairy, past fat wasps, lizards languorous with sun and wild poppies scattered like kisses onto the field.

As I pushed open the doors to the dairy, my nose filled with ammonia, brine and mould. I ran straight over to Pépé. He scooped me up, kissed my cheeks and carried me around as I explained everything to my mother.

'These are *faiselles*. They make the cheese into shapes, don't they, Pépé?' I said.

He nodded. 'And what shape are our cheeses?'

'Swirly skirts!' I shouted and he laughed.

'This is my favourite part,' I announced as we moved on.

My mother watched dutifully as rows of cheese were dusted with finely ground charcoal burned from local oak. The damp, ashen taste will forever stay with me, spilling into my mouth whenever I smell smoke, see fire.

Then my mother sighed, fidgeted inside her pocket and pulled out a cigarette.

Pépé frowned. 'Not in here, Lili.' He put me down. 'Take your mother outside.'

I led the way to a field dotted with dirty goats lolling in whatever shade they could find. Dry grass that no longer had the will to dream of rain snapped beneath our feet as I tried to persuade one of the goats to pay my mother some attention.

But she turned from the goats, shaded her eyes from the glare of the afternoon and said, 'Gaelle, would you like an adventure?'

An adventure. I turned the word around in my mind. My friend Nathalie talked of Disneyland as the place of adventure: spinning, twirling teacups big enough to sit inside; talking mice as tall as Mémé and Pépé; and rivers that flowed all year round and wound through buildings between puppet-lined banks.

I looked my mother in her shaded eyes for the first time and said, 'Yes.'

I didn't really say goodbye to Mémé, to Pépé, to my home. I didn't know what goodbye was. An unknotting, perhaps, of finely webbed threads that cling and cannot be brushed off, that linger forever and haunt you always. I didn't know that I would not see them again for seven years. That then it would be too late for unknotting and brushing off and only drowning would suffice.

TEN

I stand and stretch out a hand to Selena who is still lying on the sand, eyes closed. 'It's too hot. You'll get burnt and your mum will be cross with me.'

Selena takes my hand and pulls herself up. Then she begins to walk back towards Siesta Park. I follow, unsure. I am expecting commentary, questions, at the very least a request for more. Perhaps she was bored. Or perhaps she is happy to leave the story suspended between us; she understands that we are now both trapped in its web and we will have to meet again to tell, to listen and to finish.

But then she says, 'You don't look like you grew up on a farm. It's like your mum waved her painted nails and magicked away all the mud and goat shit.'

I think about what I have said over the last half-hour and how she has interpreted it; as an explanation of me and not my mother. I shake my head but before I can redirect her analysis, the estuary looms once more. The water is perhaps to mid-thigh now and the brownness of the sand no longer looks like sewage, but like sepia spilled from a photograph.

Selena steps forward and begins to run and splash. And, as before, she stops when she realises I haven't followed.

As she turns, I'm ready with the camera. I antique her smile and its reflection in the water droplets that sit aloft without falling, surrounding her face.

Then she is on the other side and waving goodbye as she turns to run up the path through the dunes to her house.

It is only when I arrive home that I understand Selena used the story to make me forget about what she had been up to when I found her in my cottage earlier that morning. I drop my hat on the table and begin to tidy the photographs. I wish for a moment that Jason was here to put them in albums in order, all notated and dated and shelved.

Then I realise Selena has taken the photographs of her overlaid onto the dawn light and I almost laugh because she already knows me well enough to understand that I wouldn't have given them to her if she'd asked.

I do not sleep that night. My mother's restlessness invades me, as do her stories; I can hear words whispered in the sound of the sea brushing the shore. My story, Jason's story, Aurora's story, my mother's story; all chapters of a larger tale. Who is the hero of this tale, I wonder. Not Jason. After all, heroes, like that other Jason, he of the Argonauts, are not necessarily an aspirational lot. My husband is too benevolent to be the hero. That also rules out Aurora. She is much too trusting and therefore too easily led astray. That leaves me. And my mother.

I slap the soles of my thongs onto the floorboards of my cottage until I can no longer hear the sea, but I can still feel it, the faintest pull, like an infant suckling, as the words and stories are taken out into deeper water where they will drown before they are told.

At dawn I take my bicycle and ride past Dunsborough, on and on, pedalling hard, without destination. I reach Meelup and sit a while, catching my breath and staring at rocks baked red and a sheet of water laid in perfect blue across the sand. The breeze wakes and stirs the water so I pick up my bike and ride again until I find a sign that reads Gallery, hoping to find a quiet space.

Inside, the walls are hung with paintings, still lifes, but with more still to them than life. I inspect the rest of the gallery and find nothing of interest amongst hand-painted scarves and pieces of blown glass. I am about to leave when I see a cabinet full of baby blankets, patchworked together from scraps of worn clothes, quilts and wraps. I pick one up. The wear in the fabric has made it as soft as new skin and I can see Aurora wrapped in its folds as she sleeps.

'They're gorgeous, aren't they?' The sales assistant pounces.

'Yes. I'll take this one please.' The blanket I have selected is full of auburn tones, like the soil beneath my feet at Pépé's farm.

'Would you like it giftwrapped?'

'No, it's for my daughter.'

'And how old is she?'

'She's just a baby.'

The sales assistant looks around. 'She's with her daddy then?'

'No. She isn't.' I take the blanket, put money on the counter and walk away.

The blanket lies across one of the armchairs in my cottage. Everything else is the same as it was when Selena commented on the sparseness of my belongings: beach holiday detritus scattered on the bench, table and floor. But the blanket is a personal touch, surely. It speaks of expectation. It is supposed to be wrapped around someone, around Aurora, and here it sits, waiting. I sit in the chair opposite, arms empty, waiting too. Ready for her to come.

'Gaelle!'

I am floating in the water like a ripple, watching clouds smudge the light, when I hear the shout. There is only one person who would suddenly appear like that, calling out my name as if it were a cry of jubilation.

'Gaelle!' The girl splashes through the water.

'Selena.'

'Come to Simmo's with me. Mum said we can take her car. It's the best ice-cream in the world. Everybody says.'

'Everybody?'

'Well, not you yet, but that's only because you've never been. Come on.'

'I need to get changed.'

'Gaelle, everyone wears their bathers around here. Just put on your sarong.'

'All right.'

The road we drive along is lined with peppermint trees which give way to jarrah and the occasional red gum. The trees scatter light over the road like fallen leaves. Some of the trees are dead, their ghost-grey trunks beheaded. Their arms claw at scraps of sky.

The selection at Simmo's is, as Selena had promised, astonishing. I roll the names across my tongue, taste them. Whisky Prune with Mascarpone. Chunky Monkey. Mudslide. After much deliberation, Selena chooses Squashed Frog—a vivid combination of mint, strawberry swirl and white chocolate buttons. I choose Experiment.

We walk outside and sit on wooden benches amidst happy families shaded by sunburnt gums, eating silently and basking like lizards.

Experiment turns out to be nutty and bitter and aromatic all at once. We eat without speaking because I want Selena to ask before I tell.

She finishes her ice-cream and props her feet up on the bench opposite. 'So where did she take you, Gaelle?'

❧

She took me to London for the adventure she had promised. I don't remember details of the city, such as the street we lived on, but I do remember the lack of colour: in my mind London seemed overexposed, not because there was too much light but because there was so little contrast in the city's palette. Streets, flats, steps and footpaths formed a concrete topography that my eyes, used to the Mondrianesque colour-blocked fields of the Loire, had difficulty adjusting to.

Of those early days, I remember little, but the nights are caught forever in my head. I remember the first night that I sat in the bathroom on a stool with chipped brass legs and a seat covered in purple fluff. My mother began her ritual of shimmying into satin hotpants, blow-drying her hair so that it slipped like poured caramel down her back, glossing her lips and sprinkling glitter—she told me it was fairy dust—onto her cheeks.

When she finished, she spun around in front of the mirror and said with a smile that was for once unrestrained, 'How do I look?'

Now, I would say she looked like an ABBA clone disco queen. Back then I said, 'Like Cinderella.'

She kissed my cheeks, picked me up by the armpits and twirled me around the room so fast that the air tickled my skin, making me giggle.

'Time for bed, *chérie*,' she said as she put me down, transformed the sofa into my bed, tucked me in and rubbed my hands to keep them warm. 'I suppose you'd like a bedtime story.'

I pulled up the blanket and nodded my head. 'Can I have a new story? One I've never heard before? Pépé always told the same stories.'

'Yes, he would. But a new story? Is there any such thing? For you, possibly, there is. I shall do my best.' She thought for a moment. 'Well, Gaelle, the first thing you should know is that my stories will never begin with *Once upon a time*. I'm allowed to be creative because, you see, I'm following in the tradition of the group of French ladies from King Louis' court who invented fairytales. It wasn't men called Grimm and Andersen, although they seem to have taken all the credit. But, as no one remembers this any more, it will be our secret. And make sure you don't tell anyone because, if you do, they may think you're a mad sorceress and they'll take you away and lock you in a room with spotless-shining girls who talk with round mouths, wear pinafores and have names like Mary-Jane Battersea Hyphen Brown.'

I shrieked at her silly threat and said, 'Tell me about where you're going tonight.'

'I'm going dancing, Gaelle.' She jumped off the bed and began to move around the room, humming and turning, eyes closed, head tipped back.

'Will you go in a pumpkin coach?' I giggled, wanting to bring her back to the bed, to me.

But she stayed where she was and called as she circled, 'No fairy godmothers in my stories. In this story, the princess—oops, no princesses either—the young *danseuse* dances and dances and dances all night long to break the spell and by morning she succeeds and her dress is transformed from Oxfam trash to Biba glam and her bracelets turn from gold plate to Tiffany diamonds and her false lashes stick like glue to her eyelids so that her eyes will always look dark and mysterious.'

'But what spell does she have to break?'

My mother came over to the bed, kissed my forehead and said, 'It's time for me to go. You'll sleep so well that you won't even know I'm gone and I'll tell you about the spell in the morning.'

She collected her handbag and left the apartment, her smile dancing along with her feet, while I lay in my bed in the dark.

꙰

'She left you there by yourself?' Selena's disbelief is even more strident than yesterday. 'My mum and dad still get me a babysitter when they go out at night.'

'Didn't anyone tell you stories when you were young, Selena?' I ask crossly. 'If Scheherazade was telling her stories to you instead of the king there'd only be one night, not a thousand and one.'

'Yeah, but Schehera-whatsit's stories were made-up. Yours is supposed to be true.'

'Mothers don't always behave the way they do in stories.'

Selena laughs. 'No fairy godmothers, no princesses and no perfect mums, right? I'll shut up and listen. Promise.' She makes elaborate heart-crossing gestures with her hands.

I shake my head. 'I don't believe you.'

*

It was perhaps a year after we arrived in London when something unexpected happened. I woke at the usual time, dressed myself for school and pulled aside the patterned piece of fabric that divided my mother's room from the main room. I expected her head to surface from under the duvet, her mouth to smile, her arms to open. I expected to collect my hug and say goodbye before I went to school and left her to sleep some more. But nothing moved.

I walked over to her bed. She seemed to be asleep. I touched her hair, which no longer had the glossy sheen of caramel; it was like soil, damp and muddy. The sparkle on her cheeks had gone out. I touched her arm of bone and skin. Nothing. I sat on the floor, stroking the hand that tipped out of the bed. Again, nothing. I was too scared to call out or to shake her. So I waited. Watched the clock tick until five minutes before school started. Then I left the flat with my school bag and no breakfast.

My friend Imogen was waiting for me at the end of the street, eyes jumping from her brand new digital watch to the direction of my flat. She smiled when she saw me.

As I reached her, a group of children rushed by; they put out their legs to trip me and they pushed Imogen out of the way. 'Slimy frogs!' they shouted, and ran off snickering into their scarves. I grabbed Imogen's hand and we ran on ahead of the frog-shouting children with their slow, city-bred legs. As we passed them I turned to yell, 'She's not a frog, she's Moroccan, stupid!'

When we slowed down, Imogen grinned at me. 'It's okay, Gaelle. They're just jealous because we speak two languages and they don't.'

I pulled a face. 'But my English isn't very good.'

'It's better than their French.'

I laughed for a moment and then stopped. 'My mother won't wake up.'

'Is she sick?'

I shook my head.

'Maybe she's having a good dream.'

This time I nodded. My mother was always dreaming, even when she was awake.

But once we were at school, heads bowed over spelling tests, that explanation no longer seemed to suffice. I spelled out H-E-V-N and began to worry that she had in fact gone there. The place where all good baby goats went to frolic in endless fields of lavender. That was Mémé's explanation for disappearing goats. But even then I knew that if someone was dead, they were dead. There is no sleep. No heaven. There is only an end.

At morning break, Imogen and I retreated to our usual spot beneath a magnolia tree at the end of the playing field. She pulled out a container full of soft dates stuffed with almond paste and passed some to me. Then I asked her a question I had been curious about for a while.

'Where do you think my mother goes at night?'

Imogen munched on a date and considered. 'Maybe she's a witch?'

I shook my head then put forward my own theory. 'You know that story we read about the twelve dancing princesses who go out all night. She could be like one of them.'

'I know! You could look at the soles of her shoes. If they're worn out like the princesses' were, then that's it.'

'I'll have a look tonight. Because maybe she's just tired from too much dancing.' I stopped. There was another question I wanted to ask. 'Does your mother go out all night?'

'No. She drinks mint tea with my father.' Imogen passed me the last date, then added, 'You could ask Mrs Anderson what to do.'

I shook my head. 'My mother wouldn't like that.'

We were silent a moment. Then the final pressing question forced itself out of my mouth. 'If my mother is in heaven with the baby Jesus and the baby goats then she wouldn't be in her bed, would she? She can't be in two places at once.'

Imogen offered me hope as well as dates. 'No. Besides, you would have heard the music of the choirs of angels as they came to get her.'

A bell rang. I jumped. But it was just the sound of recess ending. I just had to make it through the afternoon and then I could find out whether my mother was going to wake up. I groaned when I remembered that I had English class. That was not going to make the afternoon pass swiftly by.

Mrs Anderson wanted us to write a story for a newspaper. She said it should be factual. It should be a story about what we did on the weekends. I stared at my empty page and thought about what I had done last Sunday. My mother had sat in the beanbag and read out parts of her favourite book—*Famous Quotes on Any Subject by European Writers*. No Mother Goose for us.

'Pick a topic,' she'd said.

I thought for a few moments, looked out the window and then said, 'Lost.'

She frowned but turned to the index and scanned the entries. 'We'll have to go with lost love. That's the only thing I can find with lost in it.'

'Okay.'

'*Tis better to have loved and lost than never to have loved at all*. Alfred, Lord Tennyson. Or how about this one?

The hottest love has the coldest end. Socrates.' She closed the book and repeated the lines. 'It is better to have loved and lost than never to have loved at all. The hottest love has the coldest end. Your turn, Gaelle.'

I tried to remember. 'Hot love has a cold end and it's better to lose ... Why do you always read this book?'

'Because, Gaelle, one day you'll want to make an impression. Be unforgettable. Men love a woman who has the appearance of intelligence.'

'What's the best one?'

'*Children begin by loving their parents; as they grow older they judge them; sometimes they forgive them.* That's Oscar Wilde.'

I turned my attention back to the classroom and fixed my eyes on the story Imogen was writing, about taking the dog for a walk with her family through Wormwood Scrubs, and the smell of cardamom in her grandmother's house. Nothing about mothers who wouldn't wake up.

So I began to write. When my name was called, I walked to the front of the class and read aloud, 'I go dancing with my mother. We have shiny dresses called Biba, and if we dance all weekend then we break the spell and our eyelashes grow really long.'

When I finished, no one clapped. Instead, they stared and Mrs Anderson said, 'Gaelle! I want to see you after class.' And when she did, she said, 'I don't think you meant what you wrote. I think you may have confused some of your words.'

'No I didn't.'

'Your English will never get better if you don't tell the truth. You didn't really do those things on the weekend, did you?'

'Yes I did!' I shouted at her, because when my mother told me her stories and I closed my eyes to listen, I was there, in the middle of the tale she was telling, twirling and dancing along to her words.

I ran out of the classroom to where Imogen was waiting, grabbed her hand and we kept running, all the way to my flat, saying nothing, minds full of my mother and what we might find.

ELEVEN

My mother was in the kitchen with her smile back on, her hair freshly poured and her cheeks pink as poppies. Imogen's face scribbled over with disappointment.

'Gaelle!' my mother cried as she kissed my cheeks. 'Would you and Imogen like some *chocolat chaud*?'

Imogen nodded and we sat in the beanbag. I hoped Imogen didn't think I'd made the whole thing up; I was beginning to wonder if any of it had really happened.

My mother flitted around, pouring out bowls of hot chocolate, her mouth clattering out words. 'How was school today, *chérie*?'

I pulled a face. 'The teacher told me I was a liar.'

'Why would she say such a thing?'

'Because of my story.' I passed it to my mother who read it and laughed.

'Gaelle, it's a wonderful story. I'm going to tape it to the wall just here so we can read it whenever we like.'

Imogen looked up at my mother. 'Can I come dancing too? I want long eyelashes like yours.'

'Imogen, you already have beautiful eyelashes. The dancing is just for Gaelle and me.' Imogen pouted. 'But you can come with us on another story. How about if I make one up just for you and Gaelle?'

'But Maman, the teacher said my English wouldn't get better if I told lies.'

My mother sat down in the beanbag between Imogen and me. 'Darling, bilingual children always struggle with language for the first few years of their lives. But soon you'll know twice as many words as everyone else and then you'll be able to tell twice as many stories.'

'I'm never going to speak French again,' I announced. 'I want to talk like you do now.' I tried to mimic my mother's new, rounded accent—like she had a pearl rolling in her mouth—but she and Imogen began to laugh at my attempts.

'Oh, Gaelle, you've had a difficult day so why don't you and Imogen curl up beside me, close your eyes and let me make everything better. Imogen, you'd like that, wouldn't you?'

Imogen nodded and I recognised the bewitched look in her eyes; it was the same as that worn by my relatives as they sat around the kitchen table in France, listening to my mother. I studied my mother's hands, which waved through the air in time with her words. Were they, I wondered, like magic wands? And was she weaving a spell right here in our flat?

My mother hugged me. 'Your eyes are so big and so brown. They make you beautiful. If only we knew who you resembled.' She laughed. 'But that does not matter because I have a new story just for you. This is a wonder tale, not a fairytale. Do you remember those French women I told you about who invented fairytales? Well I should have said that they invented wonder tales, which are a different thing entirely. A wonder tale is often about a clever woman who does not belong because she does not conform. Despite that, she is lucky; there is always magic and metamorphosis waiting around the corner to bring her what she wants.

'Imagine we are in a Parisian salon during the reign of King Louis; our salon is brimming with intelligent women who are not content to be their husband's shadow. They are all wearing bouffant and powdered wigs, like this.'

My mother took her hair and drew it up high on top of her head, curling it over her arm so it looked like a baguette running from ear to ear. She looked down her nose at us and Imogen and I laughed.

'Now it is our turn to tell a tale so wondrous that it must cut through the chatter and capture the attention of every person in the room. Do you think we can do that?'

Of course we nodded.

'Then let's begin. We are travelling through time to a land of great abundance. Everywhere there are trees weighed down with fleshy fruit that drip their juices onto the heads of passers-by in a drizzle of the sweetest rain. The ground is a thick carpet of soft and drowsy roses, the sky is plump with cottony clouds, and the air tastes of honey that has seeped from the wings of bees. Each house in the kingdom is like a castle, with curving staircases and rounded turrets, and at the top of the fattest hill in the land is the biggest castle, that of the queen and king.

'This land is special not just because of its plenty but because mothers are the heroes here, unlike other stories; they alone can understand the kingdom's most treasured possession: a dribbling, talking tongue that sits in all its monstrous glory on a red silk cushion next to the queen's throne.'

'Yuck,' I shouted and Imogen giggled.

'Watch out or it will lick you!' my mother cried as she began to tickle my neck with kisses that left me helpless with laughter. She stopped when I could no longer catch my breath and she laughed too. 'I think it's just as well that this tongue is unable to leave its cushion and kiss little girls to death. No, this tongue is treasured because it keeps, locked in its buds, every possibility for the arrangement of words that lies at the heart of storytelling. Every day the tongue tells stories to all the mothers in the land and then the mothers tell the stories to their children and, in this way, their imaginations are awoken. Without the magic tongue there would be no stories; without the mothers there would be no way to pass on these marvels; and without both, hopes and dreams, and therefore life, would all vanish.'

'Are there fairies in the land? Witches?' I asked, anxious that something marvellous or frightening happen soon.

My mother frowned, disappointed that I did not appreciate her talent for telling a tale so unbelievable that it had to contain a shred of truth. 'No fairies,' she said. 'But I've already said there's a queen and a king. That should satisfy your need for archetype.'

I squashed my mouth shut, determined not to ask what an ark-type was.

'Well, if a queen and a king are not enough then you'll be pleased to know that the land is also inhabited by unicorns, mermaids and firebirds. The firebirds rule the sky; their flaring wings provide the light of the sun, the moon and the stars. The unicorns rule the land; there is no need for beer and bawdiness when one can be satisfied by the sight of the unicorns' manes rippling like trails of silver ribbon through the streets. And the mermaids rule the seas; their play causes the waves to roll and the tides to ebb and flow.

'Now on this particular day in this particular land the one sound that everybody can hear is the buzz of whispered gossip passing from tongue to ear like a swarm of bees moving from flower to flower.'

My mother leaned in closer to our ears and began to whisper. 'The magic tongue had said, in its morning story, that before the day was out, the queen would give birth once again. A crowd gathers around the castle gates. One of them says, *The queen has not yet given us a human child.*

Another adds, *She gives birth only to firebirds, unicorns and mermaids.*

'This is an important job for the queen; without her, the magical creatures would die out. But she is also expected to become a real mother and produce a real human baby. Her failure has thus far been tolerated, however it is now her fourth pregnancy, and patience is running out.'

My mother sat upright again and resumed her normal voice. 'The queen waits anxiously in her bed for the birth pains to end, for the baby to arrive. Her mother and her grandmother had borne a human child by their fourth pregnancy. So will she.

'At last, it is over. She opens her arms and then sinks back onto the pillow. She has had triplets. But one is a mermaid, one a unicorn and one a firebird.

'The queen can hear, through her window, the sound of the trumpeter announcing the birth. She can hear the proclamation. And she can hear, as loud as an avalanche, the groan of disappointment from the crowd. She has failed her people. She is not a real queen. She thinks she can hear the tongue hissing these words, words that then poison every tongue in the kingdom as they are passed around and around.

'The queen is not allowed to leave the palace; she is locked in the nursery while her fate is decided. However, nothing moves quickly when the king is involved so she knows she has some time.

'She nurses the triplets for the required time of two weeks, which is all it takes for them to grow strong enough to be released into the herds of magical creatures, so similar that the queen can never tell which ones are her progeny and which are those of the queens who came before her. And as they drink her milk, she thinks about the horn that scores her chest, the wings that burn her belly and the slimy tail that stains her arms with fish-stink. She knows that a human child would fit so well into the soft, square space made by the fold of her crooked arm beneath her breast. She selects a doll from a shelf in the nursery and sits in a chair embracing the doll. As she rocks, forward and back, her milk leaks, drip-drop. It is the sound of her unhappiness filling her up like a pitcher, it is the sound of self-pity, so she puts the doll away.

'She escapes through the window and walks the circum-ference of the world, shadowed on land, air and water by the unicorns, firebirds and mermaids. She sees that the countryside has also lost its abundance and suc-cumbed to self-pity—flowers have shed their petals, trees have dropped their leaves, the sky is grey and the air is without birdsong and nectar. Even the magical creatures seem wilted; the flare, the shine, the sparkle are almost extinguished.

'The river is so dry she has to suck water out of its cracked bed. She wonders if she could tip herself over, pour out her unhappiness and fill the empty riverbed. The ground splits and lifts as if ready to spit back her offering. But there is something hiding beneath, something reptilian with red scales shingled over its long neck.'

'A dragon,' I cried, ready to show that I knew the pitfalls that could befall a queen in distress in a story.

'Or a demon,' shouted Imogen, not wanting to be left out of the guessing game I'd begun.

It was a mistake, of course, because as soon as I'd spoken my mother shifted, then stood, extricating herself from the beanbag. She peeped at the clock and began to search through the lipsticks scattered over the kitchen table. 'Pink or peach? Perhaps peach tonight.'

The start of the getting-ready ritual reminded me of the question I had meant to ask as soon as I got home. 'Maman, were you sick this morning?'

'But what was in the river?' Imogen demanded, making it clear that a story of a queen in distress was vastly more interesting than the story of a mother in a bed.

'A woman with the head of a snake,' my mother said, beaming at Imogen who had obviously asked the right question.

'Ohhhhh ...' said Imogen and I together.

My mother applied her lipstick and spoke to us through the mirror as she set to work on her eyes. 'The snake woman hovers in front of the queen, scales flashing like a sunset, unspeaking.

'The queen cries, *What do you want?*

'The snake hisses, *To grant your wish.*

'The queen is momentarily perplexed. She is sure that fairy godmothers are usually in charge of wish-granting.'

'But there are no fairy godmothers in your stories, Maman,' I said, confused.

'That's right,' my mother replied, fastening a fringe of black lashes to her lids; they fell so heavily I wished I could part them and clip them back, then turn her face away from the mirror she was speaking to, towards me, so that I could understand the story without the barriers of glass and false hair. 'I should remember what a good listener you are,' she continued. 'Besides, a wish-granter in the hand is worth two in the make-believe story, or so the queen thinks. *You're going to give me a human child,* she says.

'The snake woman nods. *Yes, but there's a sacrifice involved.*

'The queen shrugs. She remembers Rumpelstiltskin. One way or another, queens can always get around a sacrifice.

'The snake continues, *If I give you a human child, the tongue will dry up and all the stories will stop.*

'The queen considers. The tongue has always spoken; how could it not? Then she shrugs again. If necessary, she can tell the stories. She will have a human child; she'll be able to do anything. The deal is done.'

My mother began to search through her suitcase, discarding polyester and satin and settling on spandex.

'I need to speed the story up because it's nearly time for me to leave. So let's just say that the queen becomes pregnant, which saves her from the king's wrath, and then, one day, after the requisite amount of blood and pain and wailing, the baby appears. It has a beautiful human face. Human hair. Human eyes. But there is a spiralling growth on its forehead. A unicorn's horn. The queen gasps. Attached to the child's human body are not arms but the flaring wings of a firebird. And below the knees a flapping wet fish tail.'

Imogen could no longer contain herself. 'Is she like the Little Mermaid?'

My mother smiled. 'No. The Little Mermaid is make-believe. This story is real.'

Imogen and I shared a doubtful glance and I decided to use the pause to try my question again. 'Maman, what was wrong with you this morning?'

'I was sleeping very soundly, *chérie*. The dancing makes me tired, that's all. So you're not to wake me. You're a big girl, aren't you?'

'Yes,' I said, proudly.

'So you don't need me to get you ready for school, do you?'

My mouth opened but I didn't know what words to put into it. Yes and no were both the wrong answer. I did need her. But I wanted to be a big girl too.

My mother heard the answer she had hoped for in my

silence. She ran a hand over my hair and said, 'Good girl. Back to the queen.' Then she pulled the curtain across the room and stepped behind it with her clothes. Imogen and I listened to her voice creep out over the top of the drapes and watched her silhouette dress itself. 'The queen pulls herself out of bed and makes the long walk to the river alone, unaccompanied by the usual procession of magical creatures this time, and unaccompanied by the baby, which she has left to fend for itself at the bottom of the cradle, buried beneath a pile of knitted blankets that were not designed to accommodate wings and horns and tails. She waits until midnight, the witching hour when snake women with magical powers are meant to appear. It passes. She continues to wait. Dawn arrives with the snake.

'The queen demands, *Where have you been?*

'*Stopping Cinders from making a terrible mistake and marry-ing the Prince.*

'*You useless, scaly piece of shit.*'

Imogen and I giggled.

My mother peeped out from behind the curtain and clapped a hand over her mouth in false apology. 'Imogen, don't tell your mother.'

Imogen shook her head, crossed her heart and hoped to die.

'The snake says to the queen, *I never said it would be born human, dear queenie. The child needs to learn humanity before she can achieve it*. And then the snake vanishes. Which means, Imogen, it's time for you to go home. And Gaelle, it's time for your bath.'

Imogen and I groaned. How could the snake disappear at such a crucial point in the story? Now, of course, I know that is the most likely point at which the snake would disappear.

I watched Imogen run down the street to her mother and father and their mint tea. Then I sat in the cold enamel of the bath, under the spout, shivering beneath the trickle of warm water.

My mother sang as she squeezed out the facecloth and rubbed it over my ear lobes, inside my ears and across my back. Edith Piaf's 'Hymne à l'Amour'. She always sang this to me in the bath, scrubbing my skin with the tempo of the song, her low, scratchy voice carving the words into my dreams and perhaps into hers too. Even a woman abandoned by her mother as a child and raised by her grandmother in a brothel can become a little sparrow whose voice stretches across decades to a mother washing a child in a London bath. I joined my mother for the final verse, my thin little-girl voice lost in hers, so I began to sing louder and louder until I was shouting and then we were both laughing.

My mother kissed the top of my head and stood. 'Time to dry yourself *ma chanteuse*; I'll finish doing my hair.'

I climbed out of the bath and she draped a towel

over my shoulders and left the room. As I dried myself, I thought about what my mother had said about the dancing she did in the evening, about it making her tired in the morning. I remembered that I had come up with the same answer when I had spoken to Imogen at school. Yet I wasn't happy that my guess had turned out to be the truth.

I waited until my mother went to the toilet. Then I tiptoed down the hall to the front door where her three pairs of shoes stood, waiting to dance. I picked up the first pair and looked at the soles. I did the same with the second pair. And the third. Then I returned to the first pair. This time, I pressed my fingers over the bottom of each shoe: first pair, second pair, third. The toilet flushed. I dropped the shoes and ran back to the bathroom. As I stood there, getting ready to put on my pyjamas and kiss my mother goodnight, I wondered why, if she was telling the truth, the soles of her shoes were not worn out.

TWELVE

As we leave Simmo's, Selena calls hello to a group of girls who are gathered by the counter in a state of giggling indecision. A couple of them waft their fingers at her in reply, one or two ignore her or do not hear her above the seeming hysteria of Bubblegum versus Apple Pie.

Selena sidles over to them and points at me. 'This is my friend Gaelle.'

All eyes turn in my direction and I feel like a dress in a store being given the once over to decide whether or not I am worthy of notice. I do not know what they decide because one of them interrupts the appraisal and points at Selena's toes. 'Cool nail polish.'

Selena blushes. 'It's Gaelle's.' Then she wriggles her toes and reverts back to the Selena I know. 'It'll be *the* colour for summer. Gaelle knows cos she's a beauty editor. For *Verve.*' Then she turns around and flutters her fingers in an exact imitation of the girls' earlier gesture. 'See ya.'

I follow her back to the car and wait till we exchange the crunch of gravel under the tyres for the gentler hum of bitumen. 'Friends of yours?'

'Sort of. Paula, the one who liked my nail polish, has been

my friend for ages. But then her and Shelly, the girl with blonde hair, were in the school play together so we've kinda joined Shelly's group. I think.' Selena pauses. 'That sounds pretty stupid, doesn't it?'

I shake my head. 'I remember the intricacies of high school friend swapping and dropping all too well.'

'I suppose it was worse for you, moving around all the time.'

'By the time I was in high school I was back on the farm with Mémé and Pépé. So I went to boarding school in England. With Imogen, who's now in Sydney too. Mémé and Pépé thought it best for me to be with someone familiar.'

'Did you and Imogen move to Sydney together?'

'We went on a backpacking holiday after we finished school and it never ended. We found Bondi and fell in love. We both enrolled at uni and Imogen met her husband and fell in love again. Then I met Jason. I never thought about going back.'

'I can't imagine living that far from my mum.' Selena laughs. 'I'd never get anything done. She'd ring me all the time to make sure I'd eaten and cleaned my teeth and done my homework.'

'Nutrition, hygiene and education. A mother's domain.'

'Do you reckon you became a beauty editor because of your mum?'

The surprise must show on my face because Selena hastens to add, 'You know, watching her put make-up on every night made you interested in all that stuff so you became a beauty editor.'

I take a tissue from the dashboard and wipe any remaining sticky sugar from my lips and fingers before I reply. 'It was even simpler than that. I did an Arts degree, which is not all that practical when it comes to finding a job. But the magazine I work for is owned by a French company. They offer two internships every year to French-speaking students. Imogen and I got the two on offer for our year. Then I could pay the rent.' I look at the road but the trees all look the same. 'Am I going the right way?'

Selena nods. 'But why didn't you do something with photography since you like it so much?' She points to our turn-off at the last minute and I wrench the steering wheel to the right.

'I never thought of photography as a job,' I say crossly and the rest of the ride home is comprised of silence and occasional glimpses of ocean between signs for accommodation, galleries and mansions with names like The Shack.

A hot spell has settled over Siesta Park; the air is as thick and sticky as jelly and is garnished too heavily with flies. The flies are scattered about near the cottage but as I walk across the grass towards the beach they throng together so that by the time I reach the sand my back is coated with them. I try to brush them away but they simply lift up at the scrape of my hand, hover and then return to roost on my skin.

The shore is hidden beneath mounds of seaweed; because of the still weather, the tides have not been strong enough to sweep it away. I sink knee-deep in the spongy brown piles and think of gothic tales of English maidens being sucked into boggy marshes. I turn around and walk back to the cottage, regaining my limbs, losing the flies.

The sound of giggling rises from a slight hollow in the grass a few houses down from mine. Selena is lying on her back on a towel with some of the girls from Simmo's; they all have iPods, they are all bikini-clad, they are all caught in the childish bodies between puppy fat and puberty. I wave to Selena and she waves back but does not invite me to join her group. Why would she? It seems that the latest nail polish can only get you so far. I laugh at myself for feeling left out of a group of thirteen year old girls.

As I walk into my cottage I hear the beeping sound of a text message arriving on my phone. I check the screen. The sender is Home. Jason. He wants a divorce. Or to tell me something about Aurora. I imagine a thousand possible messages that might have come from Home. None of them terrify me as much as the thought of reading the actual message. I tuck the phone beneath my towel and sit down with a magazine.

Some time later I leave the cottage again, prepared to

face the stingers that I know will be lurking in the stagnant sea, because I have been simmering next to a fan with a glass of iced water without any effect. The flies climb aboard my back and the air is scented with seaweed rot but I continue on to the water.

At the crest of the seaweed hill I see Selena and her friends at the edge of the water inspecting a bundle lying on the sand. One of the girls has a stick of driftwood and is prodding the bundle. As I come closer I see that it is a dead baby bird; the stick is tearing out its feathers. Another bird is circling above, calling and beginning to dive, but is scared off by the group of girls.

'Look, its guts are all hanging out—gross,' the girl with the stick says.

One of the other girls squeals with the delight of a voyeur at a horror movie. Another squats for a closer inspection and announces, 'It's so dead.'

Selena, who is standing a step outside the circle, points at the bird above. 'Do you think that's its mum?'

'Who cares,' the girl with the stick says.

Then Selena looks up. She sees me and her face reddens. I slice through the girls, pick up the dead bird and carry it out into the water, to a place where I can no longer stand. Then I let go and the sea cradles it in the swell, carrying it further out. I watch for some time, for as long as it takes to disappear. Then the other bird flies away, shrieking.

The girls are gone when I turn around, off in search of

another spectacle to distract them from school holiday boredom.

Dusk seems ready to fracture with the pressure of so much steam in the air. The sky oozes pink, as if the blood from the baby bird has seeped upwards from the horizon. I am sitting on one of the two cobwebbed deckchairs beside the front door, bare feet searching for a cool spot within the grass, smelling the smoky beginnings of the neighbours' bonfire, waiting for the sun to fall away, for that fracture to open up and let the cooler night air in. My phone is in my hand and my finger is hovering above the button that will lead me to the message from Home.

I don't hear her arrive; she is suddenly beside me, still in her bikini. Beneath the security light her hair looks redder and her skin more freckled. The mosquitoes start to strike at my ankles so I put the phone down, pick up the Rid, spray it all over me and pass it to Selena, who does the same. Then she scratches her toe in the sand and picks at her chin, fidgeting about like a boy about to ask a girl on a date.

'Why don't you sit down?' I say, as I kick sand over her etchings, irritated by her constant movement. The slightest of breezes begins to stir, releasing the wet weight caught in the air.

She thuds into the chair beside me but doesn't stop attacking her pimple.

'Cream would really be better for it,' I say, nodding at her chin.

'Not everyone has perfect skin like you,' she snaps but takes her hand away from her face.

'Do you feel like fish and chips for dinner?'

Selena jumps to her feet. 'I'll go tell mum.' She dashes off in the direction of the bonfire and returns a few minutes later with a sarong and a twenty dollar note. 'Mum said I should pay.'

'You can buy the chocolate for after.'

We walk to the back of the house, through the peppermint trees, to the path along the road. The holiday houses give way to homes, the difference marked by the beginning of fences between buildings, by the appearance of gardens rather than lawn and trees, by front doors that face towards the road rather than the water. Selena's house is trimmed with agapanthus and daisies, plants that do not mind a daily dose of salt.

Our thongs slap on the path and we can hear the distant rush of traffic from the highway. Selena is staring at her toes and her steps have lost their usual pace. Between us is the awkwardness of lovers after their first tiff.

'Time to leave London, Selena, and move on to San Francisco,' I offer.

Selena looks up for the first time. 'Is there anywhere you haven't lived? The only place I've ever been besides Perth is Bali. And Kalbarri.'

'I've never been to any of those places. It doesn't matter what the place is, it's foreign because you've never been and because of what you find. *The foreignness of what you no longer are or no longer possess lies in wait for you in foreign, unpossessed places.* Italo Calvino. I remember that from uni.'

Selena's attempts to unpack the meaning of my words are scrunched all over her face. Then she shrugs and laughs. 'I don't think there's much lying in wait for you in Siesta Park. Except maybe stingers. One got me on the bum today.' She pulls her bathing costume aside slightly to reveal an exact tracing in red of the filmy stingers that float in the water when the waves are absent.

'Ow.' I wrinkle my nose. 'I hope there's nothing like that lying in wait for me.'

We have reached the main road and the Gull service station housing the café that is our destination. Before I came here I would have wondered why anyone would want to eat at a picnic table with an umbrella stabbed through its centre behind a service station on a busy highway. Now Selena and I just take a seat at one of the tables while we wait for the fish and chips.

Selena scratches the table top with her fingernail. 'I wish I'd picked up the baby bird.'

A semitrailer growls past so I do not answer her straight away. When it is gone I say, 'Everyone wishes that at some point in their life.'

THIRTEEN

'We'll find it in San Francisco, Gaelle,' my mother said to me as we ate ice-cream at thirty-five thousand feet. 'Everything there is free.'

'Find what?' I asked.

'Something good. Something better.'

The early days of San Francisco did much to reinforce her words. Every morning I would wake to breakfast with my mother on the tiny porch that she'd crammed two chairs into; it was really just a landing and the landlord was continually moving the chairs and telling her that it was common property, not for her private use, but she'd unpack the chairs as soon as he'd left and we'd sit outside watching people and traffic for so long that I was often late for school. My mother would make up impossible stories about the passers-by: the woman who wore the same dress every day in a different colour of the rainbow was really a folded azalea who spent her nights lying crushed on the path at the Japanese Tea Garden in Golden Gate Park, waiting for the sun to transform her petals into cotton and her leaves into limbs. Or the elderly man in the long coat who walked his near-blind dog in the mornings was trying to collect all the different sounds of the city in his pockets so he could fill his lonely house with an orchestra of horns and clanking cable car turnarounds and the whirl of so many corner laundries.

That life only lasted about six months. It was around the time I turned nine that my mother began to search so hard for the magical 'it' that the mornings emptied of her presence. She didn't return home from her evenings out until late the following afternoon.

The first day it happened, I decided not to go to school. There was no longer an Imogen waiting for me at the end of the street. The other children used to tease me about the circular sound of my English words; they wanted me to develop a triangulation in my mouth, just as they had. But I found it too difficult to swallow.

I left our flat in the scooped out hollow between Russian and Telegraph hills at about eight thirty in the morning. I knew that if I turned left and walked up and up and up the highest hill I had ever seen then I could cut through the park and be on the downward side of the hill. I laughed as I ran almost too fast, propelled by the slope, nearly falling, perpendicular to the ground. I crossed over The Embarcadero and arrived at the piers that looked like fingers reaching out into the bay. There, staring at the Bay Bridge, I imagined the swish-swish sound of ferries and the slap-slap sound of water were the brush of fairy wings and the undulations of a magic carpet. Mystic transportation.

Then a voice behind me said, 'You live in the flat down-stairs.'

'Here's your fish and chips.' Selena and I jump at the sound of the voice behind us.

'Shit, I thought someone from your story'd come to life,' Selena giggles.

'Me too.' I reach out a hand for the white paper parcels and the woman says, 'Sorry about the wait. Busy night.'

'Let's go,' I say to Selena.

As we walk, she reaches across and tugs open the package, pulling out a handful of chips. She blows on them, then stuffs them into her mouth and gasps because they are so hot. 'Keep going,' she mumbles.

ॐ

I turned to face a woman who was dressed in black from top to toe. She held a camera at her waist and she stared down into it as she pressed a button and moved a lever on its side. Then she looked at me. 'I'm Miss St Clair.' She held out her hand.

'I'm Gaelle. Why don't you hold your camera up to your eye?'

'Because it's a camera with two lenses instead of one. I look through the viewing lens here at the top and it takes the photo through the lens at the front. I like this camera because when I hold it at my waist to take your photograph, it doesn't stare you in the eye.'

'Can I see?'

'Sure.'

I stepped over to her, looked into the camera and giggled. 'Everything's back to front.'

'That's because it uses a mirror behind the viewing lens to focus.'

'I think everything looks better backwards.'

Miss St Clair smiled at me. 'I think so too. I'm going to Chinatown to buy some fortune cookies. Why don't you come with me and then I'll take you home.'

I slipped my hand into hers, pleased that she hadn't asked the obvious question—*Why aren't you at school?*—and pleased to have found a way to get back home because my feet were blistering at the thought of facing the hills all by myself.

We walked through the dragon-topped gate at Chinatown, past stalls selling plastic Buddhas and the cone-shaped hats worn by tourists. Miss St Clair bought a box of fortune cookies and I watched the men play cards in the square until fog curled in and cocooned the city in blindness.

'We'd better go,' Miss St Clair said. 'Otherwise we might get lost and end up in the desert.'

I laughed. As we walked home I decided it was safe to quiz her. 'How come you know so much about cameras?'

'I'm studying photography.'

'Why?'

'Diane Arbus took a photograph of a boy in Central Park holding a hand grenade. I thought that picture showed just what it was like to be a child. But then I read that she said: *A photograph is a secret about a secret. The more it tells you, the less you know.* And I wondered how that could be? How could her photograph seem to tell me something and cause me to know *less* at the same time? So my camera is a keeper of secrets, Gaelle. I try to let them out in my photographs.'

'Can I carry your camera home? I like secrets too.'

'I thought you might.'

We walked along Columbus Avenue and I could ignore the shopfronts with too many lights and words I did not understand, and the vomit stains on the path, because I was so busy studying the camera. It was heavy, almost too heavy, but I rested it against my stomach, curled my arms around it and managed to make it home.

When we arrived at the flats my mother was sitting on the landing in one of the chairs; it looked as though she had been poured into it, as though she was liquescent. I tiptoed over and kissed her cheek. She didn't move. I didn't expect her to. Her vision remained loose, as if looking into time.

'Why don't you come upstairs with me, Gaelle? We can eat the fortune cookies,' Miss St Clair said.

I looked at my mother but neither permission nor disapproval were forthcoming.

'I'm sure your mom won't mind. I'll talk to her and perhaps you can come to my flat after school some days and I can show you more about the camera. Just till she's ready for you.'

I knew it wasn't the sort of thing I should say but I couldn't stop my thoughts from blurting out of my mouth. 'Why are you being so nice to me?'

'Hold the camera up to your ear.'

I wanted to ask why but as I'd already asked that so many times I did what she said.

Miss St Clair came around to my other ear, bent down and whispered into it. 'I think the camera's about to let out one of its secrets. I wish someone had invited me in for fortune cookies when I was your age.' Then she straightened up and laughed. 'Don't look so surprised. I wasn't born twenty-five years old. I was your age once.'

I don't know how, but I could see, standing on the porch where my mother now sat, a girl dressed in black with a toy camera in her hand staring at the door, waiting to be let in, then giving up and taking imaginary shots of foggy skies and passers-by. 'Did your mother go out dancing at night too?'

'No, she died not long after I was born. I didn't have a dad either, just like you.'

I almost dropped the camera. My mother mightn't have been around all the time but at least she was alive. Mothers didn't die, except in stories, and then there was always a wicked stepmother around to fill the gap.

'My mother won't die, will she?'

Miss St Clair took the camera from me and gave me a hug. 'No she won't. My mom was sick. Your mom is just tired.'

I made a decision. 'Fortune cookies sound good.'

I followed Miss St Clair upstairs and we sat in chairs by the window and ate a plate of fortune cookies between us. I broke open the last one and read the paper several times because I could not believe what it said. *Children begin by loving their parents; as they grow older they judge them; sometimes they forgive them.*

'You know that if you don't want the fortune to come true, you don't eat the cookie,' Miss St Clair said.

'I don't know if I want it to come true or not,' I said, looking from her to the fortune and back.

'Well, best we don't eat it then. We'll leave it on the window ledge for the birds to eat and then it will only come true if it was meant to.'

'How does your camera work?' I asked, eager to be distracted from a fortune I did not understand.

Miss St Clair balanced the camera on the palm of her hand. Light from a shaft of evening sun that had found its way through the fog glinted off the lens and should have cast her in silhouette, but, even though she was curled in a dark velvet wingback chair the same colour as her clothes, she didn't recede into the shadows; something kept her present in the room with me.

'The camera recovers light emitted by another lit object,' she began. 'So, right now, you're lit by the sun; you are the lit object. When I take a photograph of you, the camera steals your light and presses it onto the film.'

'How does it steal my light?'

'By focusing it through the lens and making a reverse image in the darkness inside the camera.'

'What if I want my light back?'

Miss St Clair laughed and was saved from answering by my mother's voice calling from the downstairs window, 'Gaelle!'

'I'd better go,' I said.

'Why don't you take this book with you and you can tell me what you think of it tomorrow.'

I put out my hands eagerly. It was a book of photographs. I tried to read the name on the cover. 'Albert Ren ...'

'Albert Renger-Patzsch. *The World is Beautiful*. It's about the disorder in the everyday.' She pushed me towards the stairs. 'See you tomorrow.'

Downstairs, my mother was restored. She was in the kitchen, heating a tin of soup, darting from stove to mirror to sink like a dragonfly, albeit with iridescent boots instead of wings.

'How was school?' she asked as I entered, discharging her motherly duty.

'Okay. We read a story about men who threw tea into the sea.'

'What a story! You're starting to sound like an American.'

I knew then that I was safe. That my tale had passed for truth in my mother's eyes. That she had no idea I'd read no stories, been to no classes. But I wanted to test her further. 'It's called the Boston Tea Party.'

My mother giggled. 'I wonder if there were any Mad Hatters there?'

'Can you help me with my homework? I have to answer some questions about the Tea Party.'

'Perhaps after dinner. It's tomato soup. To keep you warm.'

I screwed up my nose. 'I hate tomato soup. Anyway I'm already full. Miss St Clair gave me fortune cookies.'

My mother put a bowl of soup on the table and sat in the seat opposite. 'You can dip bread into it if you like. And I'll tell you about what I did last night.'

I picked up the bread and dunked it into my bowl, waiting.

'The things I saw, Gaelle! You would not believe me. Women in metallic dresses that looked like dragons' scales and a white horse being led by a rein of diamonds around the room.'

'I don't believe you.'

My mother stood and began to move plates into and out of the sink. 'Well, that's a shame because the things I saw were so wonderful they reminded me of that story I started to tell you about the baby and the queen. We haven't had a story for such a long time. One that you know not to believe rather than one that makes you wonder if it is true.'

I put my bread on my plate and pulled out my book of photographs, tired of her riddles. 'I've got my own book to read.'

My mother sat in our old beanbag, leaving a Gaelle-sized space beside her. 'I might tell the story to myself then, while you read your book.'

I shrugged and looked at the pictures on my pages, blocking out her beguiling voice and the memory of the two of us together, sitting in the beanbag, curled up close, stuck in a story. And the photographs in the book helped because they seemed to show a world different to that which I lived in. Everything was sharply focused, taken at an extreme angle or shot at such close range that it was hard to see beyond the patterns to the object itself. I had to adjust, not my eyes, but the way I looked at things so that I could see what was really behind the images shimmering on the pages in front of me. Without clothes and gardens and tables for context I could hardly tell that I was looking at photographs of buttons and flowers and glasses.

My mother tried again. 'Where were we up to in the story, Gaelle?'

I couldn't help myself; I had to share my discovery. 'Look at this, Maman.' I pointed to a picture called The Little Tree, which showed the tiniest splinter of a tree centred and foregrounding a landscape that seemed to stretch to infinity. But it was the tree that commanded attention; the photographer had somehow made that slip of a tree more impressive than the vastness of the surrounding space.

My mother shook her head. 'What did she give you this for?'

'Miss St Clair's a photographer and she told me all about how a camera takes people's secrets.'

'Well I'd best keep away from her then. Gaelle, my story will be much more interesting than a picture of a tree.'

'I like my book.'

'Perhaps I'll tell you about where I'm going tonight.'

'You're going dancing.'

'Dancing, yes.' My mother stood and began to gather her handbag and keys. 'With the diamond-studded white horse and the dragon-scale women.'

I looked up. 'I want to see where you go.'

'It's not a place for children, Gaelle.'

'Why can't you stay home with me tonight?'

'Because then I'll never find *it*, will I? Kiss my cheeks because I can't kiss yours; I'll smudge my lipstick.'

I did what I was told. After she left, I stood by the window for a long time, as if expecting that magical, slippery *it* to fly right by. Of course it did not and so I went to bed and dreamed of my mother whispering in my ear, *Everything here is free.*

FOURTEEN

While I have been speaking, Selena and I have returned to my cottage, sat ourselves in the chairs and eaten our dinner. My tale has been punctuated by bursts of laughter and shouts of excitement from the neighbours, who are equally engrossed in their own tale of evening camaraderie.

The breeze has died and the lawn is sweating which only adds to the steam in the air; I feel as if I could reach out and squeeze it like a sponge but it is like fog—always at the tips of my fingers and never in the palm of my hand. I scrunch up the fish and chip paper which is attracting a crowd of flies.

Selena brushes the salt off her fingers and stretches. She reaches into the plastic bag and pulls out a bag of lollipops, chooses one, then passes it over to me. I take a red one, unwrap it and lick the sticky sugar. My phone is beneath the bag; she sees it and picks it up.

'You've got a message, Gaelle.' She presses the button before I can stop her. 'Weird.' She passes the phone to me.

Who does that? I want to shout at her. I don't think even Jason would have checked my messages without asking me first. But I don't shout because the message has silenced me. A question mark. Nothing more. I stare at it. A question mark ordinarily denotes an ending, to a sentence, to a question. But Jason has chosen it to begin a conversation. I have no idea what to reply and cannot think because Selena is now questioning me.

'So do you reckon your mum saw you when you came home with Miss St Clair? Or was she that out of it, she didn't even know you were there?'

I shrug. 'She must have seen me. She called me down when it was dinnertime.'

'What would you have done if you hadn't found Miss St Clair? If you'd got home and your mum had just sat there?'

'That kind of speculation doesn't interest me. There's enough to worry about in the things that do happen in life.'

'But it's pretty lucky that you met her. She sounds almost too good to be true.'

'She never asked me anything about my mother.'

'Not like me, huh?'

I smile. 'More like you than you think, Selena. She also had a habit of popping up everywhere.'

'Except she probably popped up at all the right times, not the wrong times.'

'Maybe.' I crunch off a piece of lollipop and see Marie waving at us. 'Why don't you come over here?' she shouts.

Selena shakes her head and yells back, 'Nah, Gaelle's telling me about her mum. We've just got to a good bit.'

I stare at her. 'Do you think there's anyone in Siesta Park who didn't hear that?'

'Sorry, didn't know it was a secret.' Selena opens another lollipop and props her feet on my chair leg, settling in for another chapter.

'I thought you were going out with your friends tonight,' I say, half crossly.

'Mum knows they sneak into the pub on Friday nights so she won't let me go out with them.'

'So you're stuck here with me.'

'Yep.' She sticks her lollipop in her mouth and stares at me over her bulging cheek.

❦

Months passed in the same manner. On the days Miss St Clair went to classes, she would walk me to school on the way and then she would pick me up after her shift at the college camera shop and we'd walk back to her flat together. She'd tell me about different photographers—Ansel Adams, Dorothea Lange, Julia Margaret Cameron—and on the afternoons she had to study for an exam, she'd give me a book of photographs and we'd both lose ourselves in a world of pictures until my mother called up the stairs. The days in between, I didn't go to school; I walked down to the pier and back, I went to Chinatown, I waited for Miss St Clair.

But one night as I lay dreaming of mothers who turned into toads, my sleep was broken by the blue blue colour of lights flashing outside my window.

I heard the sound of my mother's laugh, coloured blue also, like the core of a flame. I peeped through the window. Looked away. Eyes scorched by what I saw. My mother. Two policemen.

They brought her inside the flat and I could no longer see what was happening. Then arms gathered me up. Miss St Clair. She'd heard the noise and come downstairs. She took me into the hall. My mother was there, too bright, too quickly moving, like a pinwheel churning in a gale. But when she reached the lounge room she became too pale, becalmed, dropping into the beanbag.

'Maman!' I cried, but the policemen shook their heads at Miss St Clair, who carried me upstairs.

Miss St Clair set me down on her sofa and passed me a tissue. She watched me blow my nose and I wondered if she was as confused as I about what was happening. But I knew she would not mention it. She had no mother, mine was barely there and we had an unspoken agreement that, in her flat, mothers scarcely existed.

'How about some cocoa, Gaelle?' she asked.

I nodded. Then tried my luck. 'Do you have any cookies?'

Miss St Clair laughed. 'You'll be all right, won't you? No matter what happens. I'm sure I can find a cookie or two.'

I stopped sniffing and waited for this unexpected midnight feast, my mind holding onto her words, *you'll be all right.*

Miss St Clair came back with cookies, cocoa and her camera. 'We'll open the window. I'll show you how to photograph the stars.'

I jumped up. This was much more fun than sleeping.

We stood in the still-warm night, framed by a large picture window, eating cookies and drinking cocoa. Then Miss St Clair passed me her camera. 'To take a photograph at night-time, Gaelle, you have to make your own light,' she said.

'Can I use your camera?'

'I think tonight, you can.'

She showed me where to stand and then she leaned down to talk into my ear as I held the camera up to the sky. She told me how to shoot the stars so they did not vanish into the night. She let me finish a whole roll of film even though it was two o'clock in the morning. I took constellation after constellation—Virgo, the Scales, the Argo—through the aperture and into my eyes. For the first time I noticed that constellations, when seen through the narrowness of the viewfinder, looked like skeletons with fine polished bones.

The next morning I woke on the sofa. Miss St Clair and I had French toast and orange juice for breakfast.

'I know the toast's not really French, Gaelle, but I'm clean out of croissants.'

I giggled, watched the way she poured syrup over her toast, did the same, took a bite and said, 'I like French toast better anyway.'

'Good. What's on at school today?'

I shrugged.

'Don't know? Don't care? Or both?'

I shrugged again and looked towards the stairs, hoping to see my mother emerge.

Miss St Clair passed me another piece of toast. 'Your mum's still asleep. She'll be better by the time you come home from school.'

'I can't go. I don't have my school bag.'

Miss St Clair nodded in the direction of the sofa. My bag was propped up there, along with a change of clothes.

I must have looked as horrified as I felt because Miss St Clair laughed.

'I'll make you a deal,' she said. 'If you go to school today, we can do whatever you like when you come back this afternoon.'

'Can we write a letter to my friend Imogen? She sent me a letter and I tried to write one back but I never finished it.'

'We sure can.'

I wanted to ask Imogen if my mother's nightly outings were just sumptuous tales or something more. I wanted to know whether she thought there really were places where white horses were led around rooms by reins of diamonds, whether mothers should have breakfast with their daughters, whether policemen should bring them home. I wanted knowledge, for Imogen to say what I couldn't—that something wasn't right. I did not understand at the time that it was such a dangerous, dangerous wish; that knowledge and happiness were not the same thing.

FIFTEEN

When I arrived home from school, I kissed my mother's white cheek as she sat immobile in the chair on the landing and then went upstairs to see Miss St Clair.

'How was school?' she asked as she made a plate of crackers spread with peanut butter.

'Boring. There was too much maths.'

'Photographers use maths.'

I stared at her, trying to work out if that was a truth or a lie.

Miss St Clair produced pen and paper. 'Time to keep up my end of the bargain. Let's write that letter.'

I opened my school bag and produced both Imogen's last letter and my attempt at a reply. Together we read over her words: *When are you coming back to London, Gaelle? The other girls at school still call me a frog. Has your mother told you any more of the story with the mermaid-girl? Tell me how it ends. We went to High Tea at the Ritz on the weekend for my mother's birthday and I ate three scones with jam and cream. Here's a photo of us there.*

My reply was full of unfinished sentences. I had no more of the mermaid-girl's story to share, I didn't know if I was ever going back to London and I wasn't too sure what High Tea was—a cup of tea in the clouds, perhaps. So I said, 'I think I should start again,' and screwed up my drafted reply.

'What do you want to say?' Miss St Clair asked. 'Maybe you could tell Imogen about your photographs.'

'I want to tell her about the policemen.'

'Wouldn't it be better to ask your mom about that?'

'Can you make sure I spell policemen properly?'

'Only if you promise me you'll talk to your mom as well.'

I looked from my paper to the stairs that led down to my flat. 'She'll just tell me a stupid story.'

'Give her a chance.'

We'd broken our silent agreement about not mentioning mothers and now it seemed that she'd taken over the conversation. So I began to write, to tell Imogen about my new friend who was helping me with my letter. 'How do you spell St Clair?' I asked.

'S-T C-L-A-I-R.'

'As well as light, clair means clear in French.' I giggled. 'You're the see-through saint.'

Miss St Clair laughed too. 'How about the patron saint of clarity. Which is just as well because Imogen won't be able to make head nor tail of that letter if you spell friend like that. I before E except after C.'

I fixed my mistake and then asked, 'Will the policemen come back?'

'I don't know. Perhaps you can ask your mom that.'

'So is this what you two get up to all afternoon?' My mother's voice chipped into the closeness between Miss St Clair and me. 'Talking about me.'

I looked up at the doorway. 'We never talk about you, Maman,' I said truthfully.

'No, I expect you don't,' she said. 'Too busy playing with cameras and picture books.'

'We don't *play* with the camera, Maman, we take photographs. The camera isn't a toy.'

Miss St Clair smiled at me and kissed my forehead. 'I think it must be time for your dinner, Gaelle. I'll see you tomorrow.' She tapped me towards my mother and it struck me then that I had never seen them speak to one another. And I was glad, so glad, and I wasn't sure why but it had something to do with my wish that Miss St Clair would never change.

I followed my mother down the stairs and sat by the table upon which was spread, instead of the dinner I'd been expecting, hair curlers and make-up.

'I thought it'd be fun if we curled our hair and put on lipstick. I always wanted to play with Mémé's make-up and she'd never let me. Not that she ever wore it much.'

I picked up a curler, playing along, then decided to give her the chance that Miss St Clair said she deserved. 'Why did the police come last night?'

A compact hit the table.

My mother grabbed it and opened it. 'You're lucky the mirror didn't break. We don't need seven years' bad luck.'

'You dropped it, not me.'

'You're right.' Her smile was a forced upward movement of lips that seemed drawn on her face.

I decided to push a little more. 'I was going to talk about the policemen in class this morning for News but I didn't get picked.'

There was a moment of silence. And then she was back. My properly smiling mother.

'Come and let's sit on your bed, Gaelle. I'll tell you all about the policemen. Answer all your questions. Ready?'

I sat on the bed with my back to the wall, not touching my mother, and I nodded. I couldn't believe it had been so easy.

'Well, it's all because of that strange baby and the unhappy queen in the story I once told you. Do you remember them?'

'There aren't any policemen in that story.'

'I know but ...'

I didn't let her finish because I knew that once she started on the story, she wouldn't stop. 'I've already decided that the unicorns use their magic to turn the baby into a human. And they all live happily ever after. The End.'

'It could end that way if you like. But isn't it better when you don't know the end? When you want to know and not-know, all at the same time?'

Yes, I wanted to say. But I also wanted things to be just as they seemed and to know that simple explanations were possible. So I decided to follow Miss St Clair's lead and strike a deal. 'I'll listen to the story if you tell me about the policemen.'

'Of course, *chérie*. Let's start with the story though. Where were we up to? The queen had the baby ...'

'She left it in the crib while she went to see the snake woman and the snake woman told her that the baby would be human one day but she didn't tell her how.'

My mother laughed. 'Perhaps you should tell the story. You remember it better than I do. Well, you're right, the baby is in the crib and she manages to climb her way out from under all the blankets the queen had buried her in. By the time the queen returns from her assignation with the snake woman, the baby is sitting up in the middle of the crib.

'The queen says, *So you're a survivor,* and the baby seems to nod. *I'd better give you a name then, hadn't I*? The baby nods again.

'The queen thinks for a moment. *I'll call you Desdemona. She was a forerunner for ill-fated women and I don't see how anything good will ever befall you.*

'The baby begins to cry. The queen reaches into the crib and pulls her out, tucking the horn into the crook of her neck and the wings under her armpit. The tail curls around the bend of her arm. The baby stops crying and falls asleep and the queen runs her hand along its beautiful face, sighing with wonder that she could have created something so magnificent and so ugly. She sits in a chair feeling baby-warmth spread across her chest and summons the tongue. The red silk cushion is brought to her and she can see that the tongue is grey, that its buds are open, that the stories have gone.

'Now she has three problems: how to convince the king to keep both her and the child, how to introduce the baby to the kingdom and how to explain the demise of the tongue.'

'Why hasn't the king already banished her?' I asked, hoping to end the story by pointing out its inconsistencies and have my real question answered.

'You're still wide awake, aren't you Gaelle?' My mother reached out a hand and pulled the bedcovers around me. 'Why don't you lie down while I talk and I can stroke your hair? You like that don't you?' She didn't wait for an answer but kept speaking, sounding rushed now.

'Well the king hasn't banished her because the king wasn't there at the birth. He doesn't know that his child is not quite what he was expecting. The queen is clever enough to know that the king and the people can be tricked. The snake has taught her that deception will buy you time and, if handled correctly, that this time could stretch on for years. So she tackles the problem of the tongue the next day with a royal proclamation stating that women are no longer to come to the palace every morning to hear the tongue's tales; instead they must stay home with their families and tell their own stories—fantasy and make-believe are now their responsibility.

'As for the queen, she can still remember. Stories of transformation. One of them must contain the secret to her daughter's humanity. She recounts them for one hundred days and one hundred nights, never moving from the chair, nursing the child when it stirs and letting it fall back to sleep in her arms, lulled by warm milk and magical words. At the end, the queen's tongue is also dry and shrunken and it still has not told her what she wanted to hear: if a handsome prince kisses the girl, she will be transformed; if she lets a frog lie in her bed; if she talks to an iron stove; if she peels away her skin like a selkie; if she lets the earth swallow her and spit her back out ... She knows that none of these is right.

'She manages to invent one last story, which she sets down on paper and circulates to the king and the people, about a princess so precious and so fragile that a puff of wind from the blink of an eye could knock her down, that a droplet from a sneeze could wash her away, that the sound of lips closing could deafen her. She promises the people that if their princess is left in the care of her mother, then she will one day emerge stronger and more fertile than any queen they have ever had. After that the queen continues to keep the child inside her private quarters in the palace and tends to all her needs herself, letting no one near her for fifteen years.

'Once a year the girl stands at a window with only her beautiful face showing, her wings hidden beneath the sill and her hair curled over her horn in a style that the people admire as elaborately regal, not realising what lies beneath the mass of golden hair. And so the king and the kingdom are happy, believing that there is a princess at last, unable to see the inhuman parts of her. Of course, they have no reason to think anything is wrong; because of the death of the tongue they no longer have the ability to imagine anything other than what they are told. The mothers have long forgotten all the stories they had collected from the tongue and use the morning story time to catch up on laundry and making beds and other such drudgery.

'The queen spends every day in the nursery with Desdemona, trying to discover ways to teach her daughter about humanity so that, in learning, she can gain her own. But they cannot go outside to see what humanity is. And the queen's tongue is still too withered to utter more than a few words at a time so she can no longer tell stories, nor can she explain such things as loss and war and love. She begins to think it is hopeless.

'On the morning of her fifteenth birthday, Desdemona asks her mother about her tail, her horn and her wings for the first time. *Why do I have these when you do not?*

'The queen strokes her daughter's hair. *Because I am a human.*

'Desdemona asks, *What is a human?*

'*A person with legs instead of a tail, with arms instead of wings and with a forehead instead of a horn.*

'*The people I see outside every year are humans.*

'*Yes.*

'*Are there many like me?*

'*None.*

'The queen gets up and runs Desdemona's bath, preparing for the yearly viewing. And it is when Desdemona is sitting in her bath that they make a discovery. The horn on her head begins to talk. *Once upon a time,* it says. Then her wings chime in with *there was a beautiful girl.* And her tail takes up the thread: *who was on a quest.* The queen listens, as entranced as Desdemona, to a wonder tale about a girl who is put to a mischievous test and, after many setbacks, gets her happy ending. At the end of the story Desdemona looks at her mother and says, *They speak.* The queen passes her daughter a towel and hugs her, thinking that now is the time to really show the kingdom its princess.

'But look at the time, Gaelle. I'm late. And you are asleep so I can escape and you'll have forgotten about the policemen by the morning.' My mother stood and smiled and executed a spin and by the time she completed the turn she had become someone else: there was a look of such total abandon on her face it was impossible to imagine that even gravity could tie her down to the earth, let alone me.

Ha, ha, I'm only pretending, I wanted to shout as I peeped at her through half-closed lids. But that would have spoiled the plan I'd made as she spoke because I knew she wouldn't tell me anything but stories.

As soon as she left the house, I slipped out of bed and covered myself in her black cape, hoping it would become my invisibility cloak. Then I stepped outside and followed my mother like a shadow.

She turned onto Columbus Avenue, a street down which she had warned me never to venture at night. Trolls and goblins and imps walked there when it was dark, she said, and they loved to eat little girls.

I decided to take my chances, as both the option of ending up as filling for troll pie or staying at home and wondering what my mother was up to were equally torturous. I turned the corner and stopped.

The street seemed to defy night. It was ablaze with metallic light. I thought instantly of peacock's tails and goldfish scales. I blinked and blinked but my vision could barely adjust to a night so bright it burned my eyes. My nose was filled with a musky scent, like damp sea sand or cuttlefish shells. And my ears could scarcely catch all the sounds; it was difficult to separate the running beat of heels on the pavement from the shouting and music and laughter and engines and hawkers.

Lining the street were creatures that seemed to have leaped straight out of my mother's stories. I began to think that she had been telling the truth all along; she really did step out of our flat and into a night-time world of enchantment.

Each step I took made me want to stop, to see, to reach out and touch: there was a girl like the ghost of an angel wearing tissue paper wings, her lips the colour of blood falling onto snow; there was a man with a skin of leather wrapped over his body, shining like the back of a beetle; and a couple kissing in the cinematic, spotlit splendour of the brightest night I had ever seen. I felt as if I was caught in the flashlight of a camera.

It was hard to take everything in and to keep up with my mother, who was rushing along as fast as her heels would allow, checking her watch, and I wished so much that I had Miss St Clair's camera with me to capture this Wonderland. I knew I would wake up in the morning and think I had been dreaming. Just as she was about to move beyond the scope of my eyes, I saw my mother step into a black building strung with red flashing lights. The neon sign read *The Tango Club*.

I smiled. She had told the truth. She did go out dancing at night. And this must be the place where she danced, hips tilted, arms outstretched, safe within the flare of this astonishing light.

SIXTEEN

'That's it?' Selena lets the silence sit for just a few seconds before shoving it aside.

'It's after midnight. And here comes your mum.'

Selena looks up and hisses, 'But was it a strip club or a brothel?' as if the distinction matters but then her mother is standing in front of us and Selena knows that we really have come to the end of tonight's chapter.

'Selena was just on her way back,' I say to Marie.

Marie bends down and collects her daughter's lollipop wrappers. 'Selena, can you go say goodnight to everyone. I'll be over in a minute.'

'I can pick those up Mum,' Selena says.

'I know you can but you haven't been over to say hello to anyone so the least you can do is go over now and say goodnight.'

Selena sighs theatrically. 'It's not like they'll have missed me. I see them all the time. Next thing you'll be saying, *Make new friends but keep the old.*'

'I will if you don't get a wriggle on.'

'See ya Gaelle.' Selena rolls her eyes at me and trudges off to do her duty.

'I'll get a bag for the rubbish,' I say to Marie as I stand and go inside, stalling, certain she has come to talk to me about something, possibly the fact that I am monopolising her daughter.

When I emerge she is waiting with hands full of plastic wrappers, watching her daughter kiss and hug a circle of adults who don't remember how humiliating it is to a thirteen year old girl to have her hair tousled and to be asked where all her boyfriends are. Marie winces as Selena scowls back over at her. Then she says, 'That's why she likes spending time with you. You don't talk down to her.'

I hold out the bag for the wrappers. Marie continues. 'I'm glad Selena's found someone she can talk to. But I think she forgets that you're only here for the summer.'

'So you do want to tell her to *keep the old*.' I walk over to the bin and throw the bag away but Marie keeps talking.

'She's doesn't quite fit in anywhere at the moment. Everyone here still thinks she's six years old, she's got a new group of friends at school who I'm not even sure she likes—and then you turn up. She's granted you big-sister status or something like that, but I know you'll be gone in a few weeks.'

'She knows that too.'

'But, like most of us, she's pretty good at ignoring things she doesn't want to think about. I don't want it to hit her like a ton of bricks a couple of days before she goes back to school.'

Selena beckons to her mother, clearly eager to get away. I take a gamble. 'Do you want me to ask her not to come here any more?'

Marie smiles. 'This is Selena we're talking about. I think it'd take more than asking for her to stay away. I just want to make sure she's all right, that's all.' She turns to leave, saying, 'See you tomorrow, Gaelle,' before she runs after her daughter and chases her, laughing, back to their house.

The next day I wake late. I have been dreaming about Aurora. In my dream I am dropping her off at childcare, even though it is something I said I would never do. And she does not cry because she never cries and I am the only one loving, missing, wanting.

I lie in bed for a few minutes. My skin feels hot, my stomach feels hollow and acid is bubbling in my throat. *Signs of Infection.* I remember the piece of paper that the doctor at the clinic gave me. It is still in my purse, one of the few things that has travelled with me. I read the title but not the words below it. Overleaf are the words, Retained Tissue. It does not bear thinking about. I have not retained anything.

I make coffee and sit in an armchair, keeping the blinds closed, signalling that I am not to be disturbed. The blanket I bought for Aurora is still draped over the chair and I can feel it against my cheek. I push it away. It does not feel like her, it does not smell like her because it has never been near her. On a shelf by the window are a picture book and a set of painted wooden blocks and I am struck for the first time by the uselessness of the toys I have bought. Neither are the kind of thing you would ever really give a baby. The book is full of delicately cut pop-up pictures and the hand-painting on the blocks looks as if it would never withstand biting and chewing. I think of Jason at our home in Sydney, surrounded by sturdy plastic practical toys. Both of us ready, both of us waiting.

I pick up my phone and take a photograph of the blanket, the book and the blocks. I send it to Jason in reply to his message. Then I sit down, phone in hand, and wait.

The closed blinds prove their ineffectiveness as a signal when Marie and Selena drop in—their words, not mine—as if they are migratory birds or superheroes falling from the sky. They invite me to a barbecue. It seems we are all to share Selena tonight. I say yes because the only other alternative is to sit inside holding onto my phone and the idea of a message that may never come.

That evening, as I am getting ready, transforming myself into Gaelle-the-French-neighbour, I become aware of my image in the mirror. I reach out my hand towards it, hesitantly, because it is as if a stranger has stepped into the glass. I trace the brown cheekbones that mask the pale

Gaelle who arrived here a few weeks ago. And the eyes. They seem a little replenished. I wonder what Aurora's eyes look like now. And Jason's. Full, perhaps, of relief at having outwitted, escaped and banished the monster.

I tie a scarf over my head and step outside. The air is wet with humidity and it kisses my face as I walk beneath the peppermint canopy to share a glass of wine with my wide-open neighbours.

I sit beside Marie, who is careless, but beautifully so, with unmade face, faded shorts and bare feet. She belongs to this place; everything about her, even the lines on her face, seem sculpted by sun and sea.

Selena spots me immediately. She sidles over and whispers in my ear while Marie is busy talking to somebody else.

'Gaelle, can I borrow your camera?'

'Why?'

Selena pouts. 'You're so suspicious. It's a surprise. For you. I'll even develop your photos for you.'

'I told you I don't like other people developing my photos.'

The girl frowns, her bargain thwarted. 'You know, you really should learn to trust people,' she says, crossly.

I laugh. 'Yes, I should.'

'Does that mean I can borrow the camera?'

'I don't suppose you'll stop pestering me until I say yes.'

Selena squeals and runs off towards my cottage.

Marie turns at the sound of her daughter's laugh. 'Just let her know if she's irritating you.'

I smile. 'She's fine.'

A breeze begins to waft across my skin. Clouds unveil a nacreous moon that hangs suspended on a chain of stars.

'Do you work, Gaelle?' Julie has seen the momentary pause in my conversation with Marie as an opportunity to generate an identifying sticker with which to categorise me.

'I'm a beauty editor. For a magazine. On holidays at the moment.'

'And your husband? He must be pretty busy if he's not tempted to join you.'

'Jason's a doctor. A heart surgeon.'

'Jason, the healer,' another woman says, her bangles tinkling like xylophones. 'Or perhaps the adventurer: Jason of the Argonauts, reclaimer of the Golden Fleece.'

Marie laughs. 'Gaelle, this is Trudy, our resident psychic and new-age guru. She'll read your tarot cards for you.'

I nod in Trudy's direction but do not allow my eyes to be caught in her psychic glare.

'Will Jason be coming?' Marie asks quietly, while the others are diverted by Trudy.

'No. He's working. But I needed a break. I used to live in Perth a long time ago, so I thought I'd come back for a visit.'

'And your daughter? Selena told me you had a baby.'

The words stick in my mouth; I clear my throat and hear them fly away on the breeze. 'She won't be coming either.'

There is a pause; it is noisy, not because the others are still chatting, but because it is full of all the things I could say to Marie. About Jason. About Aurora. All the stories I could tell, the maternal boasting, the list of milestones and accomplishments and extraordinary behaviour. Instead I say, 'It's hard being a mother, isn't it?'

'Yes.' We are both silent and then Marie nods as she points to a man standing by the barbecue, flipping sausages with the same ease with which I imagine Jason handling a scalpel. 'That's my husband, Jim. I met him here, would you believe. When I was about six years old. Our families used to come here for holidays and I thought he was an annoying little boy. Still do.' She laughs and Jim, feeling our eyes upon him, comes over to kiss the top of her head.

I watch them as if devouring.

To devour: to consume, demolish, use up. To take everything one can for one's self, just as I have taken over Selena with my story. Just as my mother would take me over with her stories.

I try to tell myself that it is not a bad case of narcissism, yet the stories seem to have become like my reflection in the pond. And, because I have spent so much time looking into them, I worry that I'm about to be transformed by an angry God into something inhuman. Not a flower, as Narcissus was; they are too guileless. Perhaps an insect. A giant Kafkaesque bug.

But here comes Selena. My mouth is open, her ears are ready. I shall have to take the risk and try to finish the story before the metamorphosis is complete.

SEVENTEEN

Months passed in a familiar pattern as I turned ten. School. Coming home to find my mother on the porch. Going upstairs to see Miss St Clair. Downstairs for dinner, bath and bed. My mother dancing at The Tango Club, night after night. Then, one day, something different.

I was doing my homework at Miss St Clair's table; she was doing her homework too, compiling her final portfolio as she was almost at the end of her course. She stood up to get more water but returned with something else in her hand.

'I have a surprise for you.'

I shut my maths book but did not hold out my hands. I studied the package she placed on the table. It looked safe: a square shape covered in brown paper. But I had learned to treat any surprise with caution. I pulled at one corner, enough to see that the gift was an album and then I smiled and tugged off the remaining paper. I opened the cover. 'They're all the photos we took together.'

Pictures of a night so full of stars it made me forget about my mother and the policemen; of Miss St Clair curled in her chair by the window; of a much smaller me looking out at the bay on the day we first met; of Miss St Clair licking the syrup from her French toast off her fingers; of paper fortunes flung out onto the air to join the birds, floating far away from me and my camera.

'Look!' I shrieked. There was only one photograph of the two of us together. It was taken on a weekend while my mother slept. Miss St Clair and I had gone to China Beach with the camera and tripod and I'd taken my first picture using the self-timer. We stood ankle deep in the sea, shoes in hand, Miss St Clair's face almost obscured by an enormous sunhat and sunglasses. Although I'd taken care to position the tripod to take the picture I had in my mind, I had somehow chopped off our legs from the knees down. The photograph showed an expanse of water with a woman and a girl in the foreground, stunted but drifting.

I don't know what Miss St Clair thought when I didn't appear on her doorstep the following afternoon. When she went downstairs to find me and my mother gone from the flat. I do wonder now if she gave me the album because she expected us to go; she always knew more than I did. Did my mother tell her? Did my mother leave me with Miss St Clair every day not because she didn't care but because she did? Does it even matter?

I tried to write to Miss St Clair after we left; many letters were started and then discarded. They all said the same thing, albeit in a roundabout way: nothing has changed except now I don't have you. Miss St Clair already knew that, she didn't need a letter to tell her that my mother was not capable of transformation. And I hated the way the words that I put on paper seemed always to hint at, to suggest, to dance around that very point.

At the time I was so upset I didn't speak to my mother for the whole of the long, long flight. Three things repeated themselves over and over in my mind: another plane, another land, another adventure I do not want. We stayed overnight in Sydney on our way to our final destination and I spent most of my time staring out of the hotel window. After San Francisco's languid yellow, Australia scalded me with its glare, with the spontaneity of its oceans, with the exuberance of its dirt.

'Time to lie low,' was all my mother said to me as she curled on the bed, ready to sleep off the jet lag.

'Why?' I asked. 'What's up high, looking for us?'

'Dragons,' she growled. Then laughed. 'It's time to be together, Gaelle. Like mother and daughter. I promise.'

Did I believe her? No, not then. Because it seemed as if the absences, the madness, the riddles of the years in San Francisco had finally come forth to be reckoned with, declaring that the past *did* matter and that we did not have all the time in the world to wait for promises to be kept and for mistakes to be corrected.

'I can't believe you didn't write to her,' Selena interjects when I pause to sip some water. 'I was imagining that you still visited her every now and again and took photos together and she'd turned into a famous artist or something. So does that mean that you're never going to write to me when you go?'

I laugh, but stop quickly, not wanting to seem patronising. 'Do people your age write letters any more? Aren't you more likely to send me abbreviated text messages that I won't understand?'

Selena laughs too. 'Maybe you could be my Facebook friend.'

I screw up my nose. 'I don't think I could be bothered with something like Facebook.'

'Nah, it's kinda boring. But I'd write letters if I had someone to write to. And then you'd have to let me come and visit you one day, maybe when I finish school.'

I try to imagine Selena in my life in Sydney. Creating a trail of lipsticked destruction through my office. Asking Jason too many questions. Shaking her head at the way I behaved in bars with men after Aurora was born. I try to stop my head from shaking a definite no and say instead, 'We don't really have to worry about that for now. Besides, I'm up to the part where my mother and I came to Perth. I thought you wanted to hear about that?'

Without waiting for her reply, I continue.

Perth. A small city in a faraway place. The taxi began to slow down when we reached a street lined with fake-Mediterranean houses and cottages with picket fences. I noticed only the separation, so much space between each house.

Then we stopped and my mother stepped out of the taxi, dropped her suitcase and flung her arms into the air.

'Look Gaelle! We have a whole house to ourselves. You would not believe how cheap life is here.'

She rushed up the path and threw open the front door. I stood by the curb and assessed.

A weatherboard house with the iron stains of bore water painting abstractions along its planks. A lawn full of prickles shaped like miniature brown pinwheels. A crumbling brick cubbyhouse collapsing into the back lane. The neighbours called the cubbyhouse a thunderbox and I spent the whole first week childishly sneaking up to it and tossing the door open in the hopes of catching the thunder in some sort of earthly act.

'Let's explore! Come on, Gaelle. We'll go wherever you want.'

'I want to go to the river.'

We had passed the river in the taxi; its banks were full of families and dogs and little coloured yachts. When I had seen it, I thought about Imogen and her family and the weekend picnics at Hyde Park that she described in her last letter.

'The river it is,' my mother said.

We walked to the end of the street and crossed over what was called a highway, even though it carried no cars, and stepped into a place filled with black swans taking bread from people's hands.

I giggled. 'The swans look burnt. Like they're all sooty.'

My mother laughed too. 'Yes, they're charred firebirds.'

And there with the peppermint trees parasolled above our heads and the air as weightless as hope, I wanted to believe. I leaned forward a little, anticipating what would follow such a moment, what always followed such a moment, and my mother took advantage of the opportunity to perform.

But she was not, for some reason, at her best; there was no spinning and twirling, no grand gesture. She closed her eyes, tilted her face to the sky and wilted against the tree. 'The *danseuse* has hurt her knee, Gaelle, and so she must rest. The evil beast has made it much harder to break the spell than she thought it would be. Besides, suntans, not long lashes, are the thing these days. And so she needs a land where the sun always shines, the air is washed clean by salt and the moat is so deep she cannot escape even if she wanted to.'

I had been expecting something more enchanting. Why did she have such a talent for never telling me the right story at the right time? 'Maman, I don't understand. What happened to the firebirds?'

My mother stroked my hair. 'They're gone, Gaelle.'

How I both wanted and did not want that to be true.

Imogen, Perth is fun. I eat Fruit Loops every morning for breakfast with my mother. I've been to school every day and I won the Spell-a-thon. The teacher gave me three Scratch 'n' Sniff stickers. I've learned to play 'Amazing Grace' on the piano off by heart. Maman bought me a camera—it's not like Miss St Clair's—but it's still really good. After school, I go to the shop and buy a cold chocolate milk and a bag of lollies. My favourite lollies are Witchetty Grubs; they are a worm you can find in the desert here. My friends are nice but I don't like them as much as I like you. Gaelle.

Gaelle, I'm glad you like Perth. I showed everyone at school where you lived on the map and they were all jealous that I had a friend in Australia. I wish I was there and then we could learn to surf. When I finish school I'll come and live there too. I bet your hair is blonde and your skin is brown from all the sun. Send me one of your photos so I can see what you look like now. I tried on all my mother's make-up yesterday and she told me off. Your mother wouldn't tell you off if you did that. Do you think she'd send me one of her lipsticks? Imogen.

Every day when I arrived home from school my mother would kiss my cheeks, make sure I did my homework and then we would sit outside on the verandah watching dusk draw silhouettes over the lawn. My mother sat in a beanbag and I sat on the step, wary of touching the fine mesh of cobwebs that hung from the eaves.

I turned eleven several months after we arrived in Perth. There had been no fuss or fanfare at breakfast and I worried that my mother was falling back into her old ways. But when I walked up the front path after school, I saw her sitting on the verandah in a chair, not in her beanbag. She was dressed in her dancing clothes. Her face was made-up. Her hair was blow-dried. I closed my eyes and opened them again. She was still there. I stepped forward and she waved. 'Happy Birthday!'

Then I noticed the cake and chocolate crackles and fairy bread and frogs-in-ponds. Fanta. A pile of presents. Even a birthday card.

'Sit down, Gaelle. We're having a party.'

She ushered me into a chair and piled my plate with food. Then she handed me the presents, one by one. 'This one's from Imogen,' she said, passing me a box wrapped in bright yellow paper. Inside were a Cosmopolitan magazine and a shiny pink nail polish. My mother and I giggled as we looked at some of the clothes in the magazine. 'Nobody should ever wear fluorescents,' my mother cackled, only half joking.

'What about those?' I pointed to a model strung with crucifixes like tinsel on a Christmas tree.

My mother shook her head. 'No, then you'd never be able to do anything naughty. Like picking all the frogs out of the jelly and leaving the jelly behind,' she added, nodding at the bowl my fingers were sliding into.

'But it's my birthday,' I said. 'I'm allowed to.'

'Yes, you are. Why don't you open this one? It's from Mémé and Pépé.'

I pulled off the paper. Inside was a photograph which must have been taken the day my mother came to the farm to collect me. Mémé and Pépé have their arms around me but I am not looking at them; I am looking at the figure standing at the edge of the frame, whose eyes are turned slightly away from the camera. My mother. But as I opened the present my eyes were fixed on the faces of my grandparents. I hugged the photograph to my chest. 'I miss them, Maman.'

My mother folded me and the photograph against her chest. She kissed the top of my head and whispered, 'I know you do, *chérie*.'

We did not move for the longest time. The sky blackened. The cobwebs above us began to quiver with moths trapped mid-flight to the electric light. I started to pull away, to reach for my camera, to photograph my birthday so I could send my grandparents a picture in return. But my mother's arms tightened.

'This is how life should be, isn't it, Gaelle?' she said.

Sitting there, camera in hand, content to see and not

to photograph, speaking little and needing no stories, I remember I said, 'Yes.'

But when I went to bed I could hear her prowling the house. Always inside, never outside, she walked the length and width of each room over and over like a caged night-woman. Night after night I waited for the front door to open, for her to leave, not wanting it, never wanting it, but expecting it was only a matter of time.

And it was. Soon, the night-woman broke free.

The knock on the door alerted me. Hesitant, it could almost have been one of the moths losing its way and, without the help of the light, colliding into the wood. My mother's prowling steps stopped. Stealthy ones took their place, treading a line to the door. The door opened and voices whispered, too soft for me to hear. I imagined what they might say: *Excuse me, I'm lost. Can you tell me how to get to the river?* And my mother's reply: *Certainly. Take a right at the end of the street, cross the highway and you'll be there.* Then the knocking would stop, the voices would disappear, the person would leave and my mother and I would be left safe together.

But, just as stories are fiction, so were my dreams. Instead, two sets of footsteps trod over the floor to my mother's room and one set of footsteps left, sometime later.

The next knock was different, staccato-sharp, but the same thing happened. The one after that was a rat-a-tat-tat.

I tried to compose letters to Imogen in my mind, letters about taking the bus into the city on the weekend with my mother and buying a new dress for me and a lipstick for her but all I could see was what I did not want to see—my mother and a retinue of knocking men.

In the morning I sat at the kitchen table eating my toast alone. The only visible trace of my mother was the lightest dusting of white, like sugar, sprinkled on the bench as if she had stayed up all night making fairy cakes.

EIGHTEEN

The next day I wait on the beach, dipping into and out of the water whenever it becomes too hot to sit in the sun. But Selena doesn't come. I walk back to the cottage; she is not there either. I stroll along the grass, in the direction of her house, and see her head in the garden, leaping like a flame above the hedge. I wave and call out, 'Selena!'

'Hi Gaelle.'

'Are you coming down to the beach?' As I step closer, I see that she is not alone. Her friends are lying on towels on the lawn.

'Maybe later,' Selena says.

One of the girls rolls over, like a chicken on a spit. 'We're going to Matty's house later, don't forget.'

'Yeah.' Selena nods at the girl then turns back to me. 'Maybe tomorrow.'

'Okay.' I continue walking, as if I had just passed by on my way to the shop. I reach the shop and turn around because I have no money. The girls are no longer on the lawn when I walk back past Selena's house.

That evening I can see my neighbours and their fire and their wine from the window of my cottage. I watch for a while and then check the new message that beeped from my phone while I was in the shower. Jason has sent a photograph this time. It is of Aurora's room. Something is different. He has hung a photograph on the wall. It is one of the few we have of the three of us together, taken by the midwife at the hospital. Jason and I are sitting together on the bed; each of us has an arm around the other and an arm around the white bundled blanket lying in our laps that contains Aurora. We are not smiling and I find I want to push the corners of our mouths upwards; we should have been smiling.

My door bangs open and I spin around, dropping the phone. As I bend to pick it up, I see Selena's toes painted with my nail polish, her feet in my flip-flops and her legs in a mini-skirt of the kind that all mothers want to burn because it is so close to being indecent. 'Can I wear these?' she says, sticking her foot out.

'You already are. Did you forget your skirt?'

She laughs and says, 'I hid it in the letterbox and got changed after I left the house otherwise Mum'd lock me up.' Her face is flushed and her eyes glow with teenage excitement at plans of forbidden things. 'It's pretty cool don't you reckon? I wanted to show you.' She spins around and then blurts out, 'Wanna come with us?' and it is too late; she has seen me involuntarily shake my head and is walking away, muttering, 'I was joking.'

'Selena,' I call after her but she does not turn back. As

I watch her storm over to the footpath I begin to wonder what is happening. I have been telling stories of prostitution to a young girl who is now wearing my things and who is not just seeking my approval, but behaving as if I have spurned her. I cannot tell if she has transformed me from big sister to teen crush or if my imagination has been fed by too many stories and is now simply inventing another.

I comb my hair, put on some lip gloss and cross the lawn to the neighbours' circle. There is an empty chair next to Marie. She waves at me and smiles so I sit beside her. 'Selena's gone out with her friends tonight. Some movie they want to see,' she says.

If I am going to say anything, this would clearly be the time to mention what Selena's friends had said earlier about going to Matty's house. But I realise that I am again at a loss. I don't know how to mother a child. I don't know whether I should be protecting something that has been revealed to me in confidence or whether, in doing so, I am not protecting Selena. Everything is too hard and I have become entangled once more in a mess of people and much of the mess is of my own making.

Conversation floats around me as I try to tell myself I am not doing nothing. I am deciding. It is taking too long. Now I am procrastinating. I am glad when someone slips into the chair beside me. Marie and I say, 'Selena,' at the same time.

'I thought the movie didn't finish till nine,' Marie says. 'Wasn't I supposed to pick you up?'

Selena shakes her head. 'We didn't go to the movie.' Her tone is designed to deflect all further queries. She slouches in her chair. I am not certain but think I can detect cigarette smoke, although it could be the bonfire.

Then Marie sees Selena's skirt, which she has forgotten to change. 'I thought you had your jeans on when you left.'

'I did.'

I wait for Marie to erupt, to yell, to tell Selena off. But I see how well she knows her daughter when she simply says, 'Okay. You can tell me about it later if you like.'

Selena does not reply.

Several minutes pass. Marie goes over to speak to Jim. I take the chance. 'Are you seeing your friends tomorrow?' I ask.

'No.' Selena glares at the fire, scrubs at her cheek with her hand and bends down to tug at my flip-flops. When she sits back up, the tear she has missed refracts the flames.

I want to reach out my hand to her but I am not sure what to do with it when it alights on her skin. So I say, 'Sometimes it feels like you just don't belong anywhere. When I became a mother I thought I'd finally fit in. But then something happens and you discover that you still don't belong, or in my case, that I never did. I think my mother felt like that all the time.'

'So do you.'

'Not when I was with Jason.'

'So why aren't you with him now?'

'Because I'm here.'

'With people you don't know.'

'I know you.'

'Maybe you don't, not really. You're too busy telling stories to find out anything about anyone else.'

She's right. Tonight has made me see that. I resist the desire to walk away and I say, 'I've been telling you a story, pretending it was for you. It's for me though. And I know it's not the right sort of story to tell you but you're the right person to hear it because I like you and you ask all the right questions.'

Selena swipes her cheek again. 'Do you ever lose an argument, Gaelle?'

'Only with you.'

'Well you've asked for it now. I'll butt in with every question I can think of.'

I laugh. 'Good.' I study the profile of her face in the flickering light of the fire. She is so heartbreakingly young. Anything could happen to her. I see that every day is, for her, another possibility, not a repeated pattern. And so I ask a question that I would not ordinarily ask because it is too personal, too prying, too close. 'What happened tonight?'

She shifts her head so her profile disappears and I see the hurt that is stamped into her eyes. 'They were supposed to meet me at the cinema and then we were all going to walk to Matty's together. But they didn't show up. I rang Paula and they were already there. She just laughed and said they forgot.'

The cruelty of girls has not, it seems, changed a great deal over the years. 'Well,' I said, 'now it's your turn to laugh. A clandestine party at the house of a boy whose parents are away and where everybody is only interested in getting drunk, kissing or snogging—or whatever you call it these days—as many people as they can and leaving out those who are too mature to play along. Who's got the better deal?'

She does laugh, just a little. 'When you put it like that ... Rejects unite, huh?'

I wrinkle my nose. 'Rejects is too harsh. What about émigrés? At least then it sounds like we have some choice in our banishment.'

'We'd better put it to good use then.' She smirks. 'Welcome to Dr Selena's couch. Storytelling permitted. Like what did the greatest ey-me-grey of all get up to next?'

NINETEEN

She followed her pattern. Because patterns are always repeated in this story. The pattern of woman as virgin or monster. The pattern of foolish belief in love. The pattern of mothers telling stories to their daughters. I had thought it would be up to Aurora to break these patterns in a way that I could not. But it's hard to break something that is made of blood, of inheritance, of habit.

The knocks on the door stopped. The 'dancing' began again. My mother returned at noon from wherever she had been the night before.

But I turned twelve and I had other things to think about. Such as school.

Nobody at school had ever seen a French person before, especially one who had also lived in London and America. Half of them treated me like an artefact, like something to look at, to puzzle over, to admire from a distance. The other half ignored me; I was just too hard, too far outside the circle of their lives. I had no idea what tee-ball was. I'd never played netball. I couldn't swim. These were the important things. They all had certain expectations of me: that I would dress differently, talk differently, behave differently. So I decided I would work my presumed exoticism, rather than run from it. And I would do it properly, with guidance.

Imogen's last letter had said: *Gaelle, hope you liked the* Cosmopolitan *I sent you for your birthday. I read it every month and it's the best. I wish I looked like Cindy Crawford. I've been drawing a beauty spot on my face just like hers but mum told me it looked silly. Ask your mother what she thinks, she'd know more about things like that.*

Imogen was reading *Cosmopolitan*. The girls at school all read *Dolly*; their files were covered in pictures cut out of the magazine. So, I would go one better. I took some money out of my mother's purse and went to the newsagent and bought *Vogue*. I immediately decided that Linda Evangelista would be my muse; she had short hair and did not look like the other models and that was what I wanted. And my mother's wardrobe held all the tools I needed.

The next day I set off to school wearing my foreignness along with my uniform. Style, it seemed to me, was about details. Altering a feature here and there, not changing everything from head to toe. So I shortened my school skirt and wore it with a pair of black lace socks and white heels. I kept my school shirt intact but draped two belts around my waist, one blue, one green. And I rimmed my eyes with liner in a colour so purple it was almost black. At first, the girls all stared. So did the teachers. But at recess, as I was making my way to my regular beanbag in the library, the popular girls advanced.

'Where did you get your socks?'

'What eyeliner is it? Maybelline?'

'How did you do your eyes?'

I laughed. 'It's easy if you know how.'

'Show us!' they chorused.

So, after school, I took them back to my house, happy to use them to fill in those empty hours that were normally occupied by nothing other than homework. We installed ourselves in my bedroom amidst a pile of clothes and make-up that I had transferred from my mother's room to mine over the course of a week.

'Oooh, can I try that?' Fiona asked, grabbing at an animal-print skirt.

'And I want those,' Bec giggled, pointing to a pile of oversized gold hoop earrings.

'Can you crimp my hair?' asked Kylie as she pulled at a strand of her dead-straight hair.

We launched ourselves at the pile of clothes and then I crimped their hair and made-up their eyes, using all the skills I'd learned from watching my mother get ready night after night for so many years. We turned up the radio and paraded around the room to Madonna, collapsing onto the bed in hysterics as Bec caught her heel on the carpet and tumbled to the floor in a flurry of costume jewellery.

I pulled out a packet of cigarettes, also stolen from my mother's room, and with which I'd been practising in the afternoons. I lit one and passed the packet around. I knew that Fiona and Kylie had their older brothers buy them packets of what they called *Winnie Blues*; they'd been hiding out in the toilets at school at lunchtime, showing off their smoking and issuing invitations to the chosen few to join them. My mother's cigarettes were not French—she always lamented the expense of them here in Australia—but they were, I thought, rather sophisticated: Alpine Mild Menthol in a silvery white packet. Each girl took one and followed my lead, inhaling and blowing out long streams of smoke. Bec coughed after just the first drag and Fiona laughed, saying, 'How can you cough when you're only bum-sucking?'

I watched Bec pretend to smoke the rest of her cigarette, while really letting it burn down, sneaking in only the occasional tiny puff whenever her cigarette became obviously longer than anyone else's. I wondered for how long Fiona and Kylie would come to my house, smoke my cigarettes and use all my make-up, and for how long Bec would be allowed to tag along.

Kylie finished her cigarette, jamming it into the ashtray even though it still had a few drags left. 'I reckon Toby'd ask me to the disco if I wore my hair like this to school tomorrow,' she said.

'Toby likes Gaelle,' Bec said, then stopped. 'I mean, he just watches her sometimes, that's all.'

I rolled my eyes. 'You can have him. Toby's boring,' I said to Kylie.

'No way. He's the cutest boy in the whole school,' she said and the other girls nodded their agreement.

I stood and examined myself in the mirror, holding up my hair to see what I would look like if I cut it all off. 'Toby would never sweep you off your feet like a prince in a story.' I turned to the girls. 'That's what I want. Someone who I can't even imagine, not yet, because he's beyond words.'

The girls said nothing. Looking at their faces, I knew that Toby's realness, the beige allure of the everyday, was what they dreamt about. I knew then that they did not possess my power of invention.

*

Selena shifts in her chair beside me, pulls another chair closer and lies down along the two of them. 'Sometimes I read in the library at lunchtime,' she says, face hidden by her hair so I cannot see her expression. But I don't need to because I've seen it before, reflected in the mirror when I was a couple of years younger than she is now.

'They had terrible books at our library,' I reply. 'I remember resorting in despair to the whole Sweet Valley High series for a couple of weeks.'

Selena laughs. 'You did not.' She pauses before adding, 'But maybe you'd have been better off staying in the library than hanging out with those girls. How long did they use you for anyway?'

'A month or so. Then I went all gothic on them and their mums were too scared to let them come to my place any more.'

Selena laughs again and repeats, 'You did not!' but louder this time so that Marie turns our way. She begins to step towards us, mouth opening, looking at me, but then she must decide not to say whatever is on her mind because she just waves at Selena and turns back, although I can see she is doing that motherly trick of keeping one eye on her child while the other is on her conversation. Or is it one eye on me?

I lower my voice to a whisper.

જી

My mother emerged after the girls had left. Something, I hesitate to call it conscience, made her say, 'Gaelle, I haven't been spending the time with you that I said I would, have I?'

I concentrated on my homework. I was still wearing her clothes. I stank of cigarette smoke and her make-up was smudged all over my face.

But all she said was, 'I heard you talking with your

friends. I'd forgotten you were old enough to be interested in boys.'

I didn't look up but said, 'You shouldn't eavesdrop. Besides, they're not my friends.'

I could tell my mother didn't know what to do with that last comment so she fixed on the one thing she did understand. 'You know you can talk to me about boys, if you'd like.'

She tried to stroke my hair and kiss my cheeks but I kept my head down. So she resorted to the only other inducement that she knew: fantasy. 'I could tell you a story about boys and girls. I haven't told you a story since ... I don't know ... since ...?'

'Since the police brought you home in San Francisco.'

She laughed. 'No, that can't be right. Surely it was just the other week.'

I sneaked a look at her and I could almost see her mind grappling with time, grappling with the fact that either it or her grasp on it had become so slick she no longer had anything to hold onto.

She managed a smile. 'Well, it seems I've been remiss. Let me tell you a story now.'

'I'm doing my maths homework. A story won't help me with that.'

'We could sit on the verandah together. We haven't done that in such a long time either. It'll be fun, I promise.'

I thought of Pépé at the farm, questioning the word of my mother, wondering what her promise was worth. Replayed in my mind, he no longer seemed as cruel as he had five years before. 'I'm too old for stories.'

My mother shook her head. 'No one is ever too old for stories.'

'Maybe they should be.' As I said this I looked up at her and, as eye captured eye, I knew I would relent, either because of the spell-like quality of her charm or the blood threads that tied me to her, winding me in a web so tight I have always struggled to free myself.

I followed her to the verandah—I was bored with Venn diagrams anyway—and watched her sit in the swinging chair, pushing off with her feet from the cracked wood floor, her hands fluttering about her like winged words falling into the air. Above us, pink rays of sun scarred the sky.

'A story of a girl and a boy. Let's see ... who was the girl in the story I used to tell you?'

'Desdemona.'

'Yes, Desdemona.'

'She wanted to be human.'

'I was getting to that.'

'The queen was about to show her to the kingdom,' I added, actually quite pleased to be finding out after all this time what was to become of Desdemona.

That entrancing laugh lifted onto the breeze like a ribbon. 'Of course. Well, the queen has a gown made for

Desdemona's unveiling. It is not of the finest silk, nor is it encrusted with jewels; instead it is simply cut to show off Desdemona's tail and her wings, rather than hide them in folds of fabric. Desdemona wears her hair long and straight; gone is the ornate updo designed to hide her horn. Then she is ready.

'The queen takes Desdemona's hand and they walk to the top of the stairs at the entrance to the castle. A large crowd is gathered; can you imagine them all attired in their best? The women wear hooped skirts shaped into bells by the lace of a dozen petticoats and the men wear shirts that cascade with ruffles from their chin to the floor. All of the magical creatures are gathered too and it almost appears as though a rainbow has been laid across the ground because of the colour and the iridescence of so many flaring wings and green-scaled tails and silver horns.

'The first thing the crowd notices, indeed the first thing anyone notices about Desdemona, is her face. Her features could have been sculpted by Rodin, her face painted into being by Monet. The crowd gasps and some have to turn away or shield their eyes, so powerful is the force of her beauty to people who have forgotten how to imagine that such things exist.

'But the children are the first to see. They spy Desdemona's horn and they giggle. Can you hear them mocking her? And look, they see her wings and they point. Then they catch a glimpse of her tail and they jeer. Defiantly, those parts of Desdemona work their magic. They begin to tell a story. But the louder her body speaks, the louder the shouts and the laughter of the children become. Soon the adults join in. They are not interested in make-believe marvels. They are interested only in the unreal that has become real right in front of them.

'Desdemona looks at her mother and says, *Why won't they listen?*

'The queen hugs her and Desdemona begins to cry. And the queen feels it then, the shock of the love that she has for her daughter. It is an appalling thing, a dark stain that rests in her heart; it would cause her to do anything, to pull out the heavy stones from the walls of the castle and hurl them into the crowd until one by one her people lay down dead at her feet. She sees also, in the eyes of her daughter, a need so strong it is almost greed. Desdemona wants this love; she covets it. She thinks it can smother the laughter, silence the taunts, sweep the hurt away.

'It becomes suffocating; the queen can no longer bear the weight of such a love because it is crushing her and she is losing her voice. So she turns to her daughter and does the only thing she can; she opens her mouth, stretches it wide and sucks Desdemona inside her with one swallow. Then she runs back to the river where the snake woman appeared to her so many years before and she spits Desdemona out into the water. *Now you will learn what you need to know,* she cries and leaves before her daughter has the chance to understand what her mother has done.

'Desdemona floats in the water for some time. Her head feels empty; her astonishment at being swallowed and spat out has caused her to temporarily forget who she is. Her mind seems to have attached itself to her wings or her tail or her horn because all she can hear are fragments of stories. In one of these a snake woman appears and tells her that to learn the secret to humanity she needs a helper, and that her helper will be the next person she sees.

'The next person she sees is a boy called Hero. The boy had watched Desdemona's presentation to the kingdom that morning and he did not heckle or laugh because he could not speak. He had to leave because to look at her was to feel like weeping but then he returned because to not see her was more than he could bear. So he followed the queen to the river and watched her disgorge Desdemona. Now he can hear a howling sound, like a thousand voices baying for blood, and he knows the people of the kingdom have come to find Desdemona, to destroy this creature they cannot understand.

'He jumps into the water and helps her swim downstream to a cave he knew when he was a boy fishing in the river for tadpoles, tadpoles that always died before they could turn into frogs. The two huddle in the cave without speaking until the wailing sound passes by.

'Hero is the first to speak. *You can't go back.*

'*Why not?*

'*They're afraid of you.* Hero's words have the inflection of truth that only someone who has never heard stories will possess.

'*But I'm a princess.*

'Hero stands. *Not the kind they were expecting. You need some clothes.*

'Desdemona realises that she is wet and that she is supposed to follow him. She takes a few steps then stops. *Why are you helping me*?

'Hero continues walking; she cannot see his eyes. *Who else will?* His words do not have the same trace of truth that they did before and the girl wonders what it is that he is afraid of telling her.'

I sighed. 'Does he love her? Is that what he doesn't want to say?'

'Of course. This is a story with a boy and a girl. What other explanation could there be?'

I wished I hadn't asked. I found I preferred the story without my mother's style of explanation and resolved not to interrupt again.

'Hero leads the way back to the castle. They travel at night, keeping to shadows and undergrowth, unknowingly aided by the magical creatures who want the princess who possesses all of their best features to succeed. The unicorns canter around them, creating an enchanted circle that cannot be broken, the firebirds fly overhead, obscuring the moon and blanketing the boy and the girl in the safety of darkness, and the mermaids stage a spectacle in the surrounding sea so that people are drawn to watch them and to forget for the moment all about their imperfect princess.

'When they reach the castle, Desdemona performs a hop on her tail and a flap of her wings to lift herself onto Hero's shoulders and clamber through the window of the nursery. She finds some clothes and drops her wet dress on the floor. As she is about to leave, the door opens. She has just enough time to hide behind the curtains.

'In walks the queen. She does not turn on the light. She sits in the rocking chair where she once nursed Desdemona. In her hands is a cushion. On top of the cushion is a wet, red tongue, quivering with fifteen years worth of untold stories. It seems that the snake woman has given up on the girl and has restored the tongue to its former power. But it also seems that the queen is not happy to accept this exchange. She is squeezing the tongue in her fist and Desdemona can see, leaking from the tongue, not blood, but an endless stream of words. *Desdemona does not need your stories*, the queen says as her hand presses tighter, *she will make her own.*

'Now it is Desdemona's turn to feel it: the shock of love. She understands that forgiveness is not in question—her mother may have swallowed her up and spat her out but she will always, regardless, be under the spell of this love.

It is not a perfect thing; it is the hardest thing, it is full of such moments, where the wish to leave the other is as strong as the need to stay.

'Then the strangest thing happens. Desdemona's tail begins to shrivel. The scales become a powder of green glitter that sparkles on the floor beneath a pair of feet, a pair of legs. *Look Mama,* Desdemona cries out but, in her excitement, she has not noticed that her mother has left the room and is unaware of the small miracle occurring in the nursery.

'Desdemona turns towards the window but her legs stagger beneath her like a newborn foal's. *Hero,* she whispers into the night and suddenly he is there beside her, holding her hand, helping her to balance, making his body into a ladder for her to climb down into the garden below.

'He smiles and points at her beautiful legs. *I thought you were just going to change your clothes.*

'She laughs and pulls him along behind her, getting the feel of her new limbs. *Now we can run.*

'And they do, all the way back to the cave, where she tells him about the bargain struck with a snake by her mother long ago. *Perhaps soon I will have arms and a smooth forehead too. I will be like everyone else.*

'As soon as the words are out of her mouth she wonders if that is really what she wants but she has no time to think of it because Hero is brushing her hair from her face and saying, *You're too beautiful to be the same as everyone else.*

'That night, as Hero and Desdemona lie together and watch unicorns fly across the face of the moon, Desdemona's horn and wings begin to tell a story. Without the tail, every third sentence is missing, and so the tale becomes both more cryptic and more fascinating because of what is left out. Hero and Desdemona take it in turns to fill in the absent sentences but then stop and listen and imagine instead.'

My mother paused and her eyes were closed. 'Could you get me a glass of water, Gaelle?' she asked.

As I filled the glass at the sink I could see her, through the window, rocking gently in the chair. It should have been an image of repose but it was not and I wanted to know what it was about the way she was composed that made me see edginess, something unable to settle. Or perhaps it was my own restlessness that I felt. The story was not going where I'd thought it would. It was not so wondrous any more; mothers did not consume their daughters and I wanted to go back to the beginning with the talking tongue and the unhappy queen and the magical creatures and deal with them in a more familiar manner.

I picked up my camera on way back outside and focused, adjusting the f-stop to allow for the lack of light. Then I took my mother's picture. I don't know if it was because her eyes were closed and I could not see inside her but even as I took it I knew I wanted something more substantial. I wanted to lift her lids and see what lay at the bottom of her eyes.

She seemed to know when I had finished and began to speak again.

'When the story told by the magical pieces of Desdemona finishes, Hero and Desdemona are quiet for a while and then she turns to find him looking at her with his love flickering in the curve of his open eyes. She stretches out her hand. He moves closer and touches his lips to hers. That night, their souls meet.'

'You mean they have sex.'

My friends' mothers would have gasped. My mother just opened her eyes and I saw it then, the substantial thing I had been searching for, but I also saw that it was comprised of gradations of shadow too intricate for the camera to copy on to film.

'Yes, Gaelle,' she said.

I looked away and did not photograph the thing I had wanted to take.

'Desdemona and Hero lie wrapped in one another's arms and he soon falls asleep. But she is wide awake. Because this love that she has for Hero, which she knows is the kind of love she has heard about in story after story, is no great and shocking thing; it is more of a tremble, a slight quiver. A fine feather stroked over her heart and through her mind. She cannot understand why this love commands so much attention when it is the other love she felt for her mother this evening that tears at her like a bird scratching for worms.

'By the morning, there is another feeling inside her. Her hands move to her stomach. Something is moving in there, coming to life. She turns to tell Hero but her words are drowned out by the voices of the entire kingdom, combined in a war cry, not too far away.'

I shivered. 'I'm going inside.'

My mother nodded her head and did not move.

TWENTY

I look at my watch and am surprised to discover it is midnight. Selena has fallen asleep. I watch alabaster shards of moonlight splinter over her face until Marie steps over and lifts her daughter's head, placing it into her lap.

'Telling Selena more about your mother?' she asks and I don't know why but I want so much to hear the version of my tale that comes out of Selena's mouth and into Marie's ears. All I say to Marie though is, 'Yes.'

'There are lots of women who still feel like mothers even though others don't think they are.'

I look away from her daughter, towards the bonfire, which is dying out, and say coldly, 'You mean my mother.'

'Not just her.' Marie pauses, then strokes her daughter's hair, tucking a loose strand behind the curve of her ear. 'After Selena was born I wanted to leave so many times. She had reflux and she cried almost without stopping for month after month. I didn't give myself any space just for me; I thought that to be a good mother I should have her attached to me all the time. I ended up in hospital with postnatal depression. People didn't talk much about it back then. My friends thought I'd abandoned my child, that I wasn't a real mother. But for me it was the only thing to do; to leave for a while. Sometimes you just don't have any more love left to give away.'

I try to imagine Aurora attached to me. I try to imagine her crying. But I can't hear the sound of her voice; I don't know if it is sharp like a cat's or a low bleating like an abandoned kid, and the frogs are shrieking too loudly, the possums scratching too roughly overhead for me to hear her imagined voice. Then clouds shroud the moon and Selena's face darkens. The bonfire is blown out by the wind. Marie is invisible. So am I. *Sometimes you just don't have any more love left to give away.* In the dark at Siesta Park, Marie's confidence echoes in the air more fully than the wind, the possums, the frogs. Only I can hear it. And, unbidden, the images whirr.

Steel barred bed. Nurses flirting with the anaesthetist: *Barry, we missed you at drinks last night.* Barry smiling, pleased at the attention. Epidural in, first piercing of the body. Faces: nurse, doctor, anaesthetist. No one I knew. I couldn't do this alone. Catheter. Second violation. It was not my body any more, it was theirs. A thing I happened to be attached to by a distended belly. Shaving. Third transgression. Stripped and stabbed and flushed. Clean. Pure. Virginal. A mother. Nearly. But I wasn't up to the caesarean in prenatal classes. I didn't know what to do. I was supposed to be having a proper birth. Push the baby out, kneeling on all fours in a birthing suite; Jason there rubbing my neck, reminding me to breathe. Something to tell people about. Ten-hour labour, the only complication a little vomiting from too much gas. Someone to love at the end of it. Then a screen went up. Green cloth. It truly was not my body. I could not see it any more. Blinded. I was on one side with my head and shoulders. Everyone else was on the other side with their whole bodies. My legs were numb. I could hear shouting. No more flirting. Someone was tense. Me? They pulled me apart, tore me open, ripped something out of me. Jason. At the door. He didn't see me see him. He saw what they dragged out of me, turned around and left. What had I done? Didn't eat properly? Worked too hard? Didn't love enough? Doctors, nurses, everybody turned away from me. Moved to a corner with my baby. Not mine any more. Aurora.

Then the clouds move on, the images dissolve and I am still sitting in a plastic chair beside a spent fire looking down at the face of a girl in her mother's lap.

PART IV

TWENTY-ONE

The next day the weather changes. The sun and sand no longer burn. The clouds are grounded. Too heavy to fly, they smother me with liquid air, compress my world to claustrophobia. I sit by the sea regardless, willing it to calm, willing windows of blue sky to open, pockets of cloud to empty. My mind is congested with words, sticky with meaning like a lungful of phlegm.

There is nothing to see but a yacht at rest. If I squint a little, it could be a pelican with head dipped. I can hear, in the abandoned water, echoes of children.

It cannot logically be so. But I no longer believe in logic, the absoluteness of one thing causing another. Life is, it seems, a random, shifting jigsaw whose pieces obey no laws, act without plan and throw up only the unexpected.

But the girl, the girl defies my musings with her usual call, her expected interruption. 'Gaelle!'

I stay where I am and she skids down the sand with the requisite degree of flurry and spirit.

'Everyone's *napping*. I'm bored. Here's your camera.'

'Finished with it, have you?'

'Yep.'

'What are you up to, Selena?'

'I'll tell you if you tell me why you came to Siesta Park,' she says.

'I told you last night.'

'Because you need to tell a story to me. But you didn't know me when you came so that's not why you're here.'

'Well I won't tell it to you any more then.'

Instead of responding to my childish retort with one of her own she reverts to my original question. 'I borrowed your camera because I'm organising a surprise for you.'

I am so startled by the notion of a surprise that I can't even respond. Selena uses my silence to dart away, waving and shouting, 'I'll show you soon!' And then she is gone.

It is afternoon and I have closed myself in the cottage. My camera feels too heavy to lift, my legs too tired to move. I turn on my phone and select a photograph I took that morning, then send it to Jason. It is of the grey sky smothering the grey sea, suffocating all traces of blue from the water. Then I dial my message bank, press loudspeaker, place it on the table and stand in the kitchen looking out at the sea while voices from my past fill the room.

'Gaelle, I don't know what to say any more except that we all miss you. Come home. Talk to Jason. You always said you didn't want to be like your mother but running away is exactly what she'd do.' Imogen's voice. Trying tough love. But then, Imogen believed in self-help and other ridiculous philosophies.

Rehana has apparently decided that enough time had passed and it is now appropriate to call. '*Chérie*,' she coos. 'Launch parties aren't the same without you. Have you seen how badly your replacement writes?'

Margaret, my mother-in-law, has not, it seems, discharged her duty in her earlier phone message and is, for some reason, persisting. 'Gaelle, please call Jason.' That is it. I wonder why she has suddenly become so succinct.

Mémé and Pépé offer love.

There are no more messages. I run through them again to make sure I have not missed one. I am halfway through when I start to feel watched.

Marie is standing at the door. The girl is hovering at her side, like a bee about to sting, and she mouths, *Sorry*, at me. I turn the phone off.

'Can we come in?' Marie asks.

I don't bother to answer as there is no need; they are virtually inside already.

'I've got some invites to the launch of the photography exhibition I told you about,' Marie says.

I stare at her and shake my head, wondering what she is talking about.

Selena interrupts. 'You know, Gaelle. I gave you the flyer. I told Mum we had to take you.'

Marie passes me a piece of paper. *Floating in the Light*, it is headed. I notice the date. Tomorrow. 'I can't.' I pass the ticket back.

'You have to.' Selena hops from one foot to the other. She is still wearing my nail polish on her toes. 'It's your surprise.'

'I hate surprises.'

'If you'd just said you'd come then I wouldn't have had to tell you it was your surprise and then you wouldn't have decided to hate it already,' Selena says crossly.

I almost cannot help but laugh at her logic. So I look neither at Marie nor Selena, but through the window at the pixels of my life. Sea. Sand. Sky. A surprise. The stolen photos. The borrowed camera. An exhibition. I don't want to know what it all means because I'm sure it can't be good.

Then the girl cuts across my vision and I turn to her at last. 'I also hate exhibitions. Photographs hung, spotlit, on view.'

'You're supposed to look at photographs, Gaelle. That's the whole point of them.' The girl flounces out of my cottage. Her mother sighs and follows. I lock the door behind them.

Rain has started to fall, throwing Siesta Park, this place of light, into unexpected darkness. People no longer know what to do with themselves. They stand on their decks in shorts and thongs, holding cups of coffee and watching water run from the clouds. They flow outside as soon as a rainbow stacks colour on to the sky but trudge back in as the world begins once more to dissolve in a deluge of liquid grey.

I take out my bike and cycle into town, regardless. It does cross my mind, just once, to cancel the appointment. But the things I have put off are printed across my every thought; they have not, as I had hoped, become less insistent through lack of action.

The medical clinic is dreary and full of illness. I tell my story to the doctor and then lie on a table with my legs apart while he places one hand inside me and one against my stomach. He wants to find something wrong, to punish me for swimming and for having the check-up too late and for doing all the things that the nurse at the abortion clinic told me not to do. But apparently there is nothing wrong; I have healed. The ending I chose is a happy one.

The doctor turns his back to me—I wonder at this belated attempt to restore my privacy—as I climb down from the table. I refuse the information he would like to share regarding contraception. 'It's no longer necessary,' I tell him, then leave.

I return to my cottage. As I lean the bike against the wall I see a shadow move across the planks. I don't look up.

'So just tell me one thing. What's the point in taking photos if no one ever gets to see them?' Selena asks.

I walk inside but of course she follows. So I give her the

shortest answer I can. 'It's just as Miss St Clair explained: a *photograph is a secret about a secret*. People at exhibitions never see that.'

'Who cares if they just see the photo and nothing else? If it's a secret, then you don't want them to see it anyway.'

I do not bother to reply, which is a mistake. Selena pounces on the silence. She gestures to the blanket and toys I bought for Aurora. 'And why do you buy all that stuff for Aurora but never send it to her?'

'All mothers buy presents for their children.'

'No, all mothers *give* presents to their children.'

The girl is looking at me and I can see in her eyes the latent image of an exposure yet to be developed. Hero worship. She doesn't yet know that, as Nietzsche said, the hero is both an affliction and a terror.

'You're too young to understand,' I say, which is, of course, the worst possible thing to say to a thirteen year old girl who thinks she knows everything and who still believes that treachery and betrayal only happen in stories.

She turns away and leaves. The look in her eyes has developed to include a trace of understanding about who I really am.

Now that the girl will no longer speak to me, I have been left alone. Which is, of course, what I wanted. Because I do not have all the time in the world. My lease expires in two weeks. My cottage has been let to somebody else.

As always, there is an interruption. This time, a tapping on the door. I look up, hopefully, because I do not expect such restraint from my neighbours, although how I expect Jason to locate me from a photograph of a beach is unclear. It is Marie.

'Gaelle, I know there's something going on that you don't want to talk about but now Selena's really upset. She was just trying to help, to organise something she thought would be fun.'

A mother protecting her daughter. I know it is only natural. She can't help it. But I'm not in the mood. 'I don't need any help.'

'Don't you?' Marie tries to catch my eyes. I don't let her.

She persists. 'If you don't need any help and nothing is wrong then why are you hiding away in Siesta Park when your family is over in Sydney?'

'I don't need mothering, Marie.'

'Well you need something. You can't just unload all your stuff on Selena and do nothing for her in return.' Marie hesitates and I can see her grappling with her next words: how to say what needs to be said and doesn't want to be said. 'She's almost infatuated with you. You know she is and I'm starting to think you're just using her to serve your own purpose.'

No, I want to shout. *I'm not that person. I know that person but she's not me.*

Marie waits for me to respond, but only because politeness comes to her as naturally as evasion comes to me. She shakes her head. 'Gaelle, we're still going to the exhibition tonight. It would be the decent thing for you to come and see the surprise that Selena's organised.'

Then she leaves. For the second time in a day I am left with a vision of a retreating redhead.

I walk down to the beach. I want something solid. But even the sea betrays me. It is like a fantasy. Surely nothing can be this perfect. I cast my eye over sand, water and sky, searching for the layer of darkness. But all I see is light.

I walk and walk and then I stop and stand on the curve of the bay, too close because the water laps my toes. I can feel something—perhaps it is the day—lying about me, broken into pieces. My mind recalls standing on another shore, poised, before, with Jason. I wonder if this is another before and, if so, what will come after.

Dusk begins to drop over the sky, smudging the light. I turn away and go back to the cottage. Marie's car is there, waiting to take me to an exhibition I do not want to see.

It is the only time I have ever seen Selena dressed in anything other than a bikini and sarong or shorts. She is wearing a green dress and her hair is washed and blow-dried and beautiful. Her face, when she looks up at me, is almost regal and I see that I cannot call her a girl any more. But I understand that the girl with the childhood worth preserving will always be there, beneath everything. And that whatever has happened over the past couple of months, whatever I have thought or imagined or was actually real, she is my friend and I am hers and it as simple as that. Of all of us, Selena has the strength to handle anything.

I look down and clutch my sarong. 'I'm not dressed. I can't wear a bikini into town.'

'We can wait for five minutes,' Selena says.

I hesitate in the space between going and staying. Selena laughs. 'Doesn't just one little part of you want to come and see what the surprise is?' she asks.

'I really don't know,' I say, honestly.

'Remember how Miss St Clair said that the reason she took photos was to let the secrets out. That's what you used to do. With your mum. But now they're all stuck like a big glob of gum in your camera. That's why I want you to come.'

'Isn't there an easier way to remove globs of gum from cameras?'

Selena rolls her eyes at me. 'You told me that the truth was always there in the photograph. Maybe you're just too scared to come and see.' Her stare and her eyes dare me, just as they did the first time we met, when I photographed her jumping from the trampoline up into the sky.

And again I do what it is that she wants. 'Okay. Give me a few minutes to change.'

TWENTY-TWO

As we drive to the town hall, I stare out the window but see nothing. I tug at the hem of my skirt. It feels too much, too concealing, in this place of bikinis and thongs, as if I have been cast into a naked Eden, fully clothed.

No one is speaking and I feel, for some reason, like a naughty child being given the silent treatment. Selena is scrunched over to her side of the car. Marie looks at the road. The radio is not turned on. The windows are closed and even the hum of car tyres is barely discernible. My mouth spills words to quell the quiet.

'Selena, you can tell me what's going on now. And don't expect too much; maybe I won't be as surprised as you think.'

Selena turns to me and mimics my officious tone. 'Gaelle, it wouldn't be a surprise if I told you. And I don't expect anything of you; if I did, I would have given up on you ages ago.' She pokes out her tongue and begins to laugh.

I laugh too. My throat, once released, fills with words. 'I think I lied to you though. The truth is not always there in the photograph. I found that out at school when I developed the photos I'd taken of my mother sitting on the porch.'

Selena unscrunches herself and asks, 'What'd they turn out like?'

The car comes to a stop. 'We're here,' says Marie and there is no way I can reply to Selena as we leave the car and cross the bitumen to the exhibition hall. Several people are gathered on the lawn outside, drinking wine. A woman waves at Marie and says, 'One of the photos decided to launch itself off the wall just before we opened. So we thought we'd have drinks out here till they finish rehanging it. Should only be about half an hour.'

I say to Selena, 'See, maybe it's an omen. I'm not meant to come.'

'Yeah right. You're not getting out of it now.'

Marie continues to chat to the woman so Selena and I move to sit on a low limestone wall which borders a bed of roses beneath a peppermint tree. The grass is cool on my feet, the wall is cool on my legs and the long-fingered leaves of the tree reach down and brush against my neck.

Selena's earlier question reverberates in the evening air and I think about Marie's words before I answer her. But something has shifted; it is no longer about me telling, it is about both of us wanting to find out what happened. I close my eyes, trying to see those pictures of long ago.

The photographs showed a beautiful child-woman rocking back and forth in a swing-seat, eyes closed, possibly asleep. Her mouth was slightly open as if singing or kissing the air and the stillness of her face cast her as a figurine: fixed, tranquil. I had set the f-stop just right; the background was blurred and my mother was clearly in focus so I could not blame my inability to see on a technical problem. It was just that, at the time, I did not yet care to look.

I studied them as I walked home from school the long way, by the river, because I wanted to be certain that my mother would be home by the time I arrived. I expected to see her sitting on the front step, staring at nothing. But she wasn't there.

I looked in each of our four rooms and then braved the walk through the knee-high straw—it had long since given up being lawn under our care—to the outhouse. Not that I really thought she'd be there. We avoided the outhouse at all costs.

I pushed the door but it was stuck. Or something was leaning against it on the inside. I called out. No answer. I bent down onto my hands and knees, like a baby, and tried to peer through the hole left by the snapped door slats. I could see only darkness. I poked my fingers through the hole, shut my eyes and felt around. Sand. Rocks. Something like hair tickled me and I pulled my hand out so fast I fell back into the grass. I flapped my fingers and shrieked and a spider that seemed as big as a baby goat flew off and scuttled away. I shivered and called out again.

'Gay-ill!' I stood up. It was Baa-arb, our neighbour, whose brassy accent flashed off my name and rendered it someone else's. She was dressed, as usual, in boisterous florals, had a baby in her arms and a crowd of children trailing behind.

'Your mum's not home. Haven't seen her come stumbling up the path yet.'

I stood up, straightened my skirt and rounded my mouth so my accent was the exact opposite of hers. 'I just remembered that she's out buying presents for me. I'm thirteen today.'

Barb laughed.

I turned and ran, chased away by her relentless cackle. As I neared the house I smiled; a light was on and she was home and there'd be cake and candles and perhaps a present or two.

But when I stepped inside, I found that the light I'd dreamed into being was just a globe of setting sun strung up outside the front windows, spilling forth a single beam onto the photograph I had taken of my mother. I grabbed the curtains and wrenched them shut, wanting to turn off that spotlight but I could still see the photograph, see the careless pose my mother wore so comfortably, like pyjamas. I studied her for a moment, wanting to find all the things that made us different. But there was only hair the same colour as mine and a set of lips with the top too thin and the bottom too full, just like I saw in the mirror every day. So I knocked the photograph to the ground, pushed my heel through the paper and pulled a chair into the cupboard in my mother's room. I felt along the top shelf until I found the jar I'd seen her hide behind a pile of Glomesh bags. It was not as heavy as I'd expected it to be and when I pulled it down I could see it was nearly empty, no longer full of money but rattling with a few lonely silver coins. I took off the lid and counted. Two dollars. It would be enough.

I searched some more, through piles of lycra and plastic earrings, but the only present I found was a sealed box from Mémé and Pépé. I stepped down, put the coins in my pocket and left the present on my chair in the living room. Then I walked down to the river, eyes fixed to the kiosk, shutting out any peripheral visions of contented families sprawled like flies over the grass, eating fish and chips and licking ice-cream. I ordered a serve of chips and went back home.

There was one last flicker of hope as I waded through the grass to our verandah. I stumbled, tripped over something large and firm, so I bent down slowly, both wanting and not wanting it to be, pushing aside long leaves of grass, peering into the darkness. It was only a plank.

I wanted to wring myself dry, to squeeze out every last drop of hope because if I had no hope, I could not be disappointed. But dreams are so hard to seize in the palms of your hands; they resist compression and seem instead to feed and grow stronger when you most need them to breathe their last.

I went inside and sat on my chair with my grandparents' gift on one knee and the package of chips on the other. In between mouthfuls, I opened the present and found a letter for me, a letter for my mother, and two books, one of Cartier-Bresson's photographs, the other the next volume of Colette's Claudine novels. I opened the letter to my mother first, stared at the cheque inside and read Mémé's words congratulating her on her new job as a secretary for a company with a big office in the city. Words about how nice our house on the river sounded, with its rose bed and kitchen garden. Pleas for her to bring me to France for a visit. Here was a cheque for the tickets. Sorry she'd not received the money in the last letter. Seven years was too long to be apart. Wouldn't we come home?

I pushed the books and the letter aside and sat in the dark, closed space of the living room with moonlight reflecting off my face and casting me against the wall as a fiercer, more robust creature. I felt life invert. Everything was about to change.

I heard the sound sometime later, not a sob, not a sigh, but a gasp: a person drowning. The light of the moon, filtered by fast moving cloud, flickered blue.

I did not move straight away; it was after midnight and time no longer mattered and I knew I could not change, by moving more quickly, what had already happened.

The child-woman sat on the verandah, body still immobile but fixed in a pose that spoke more of violence than tranquillity. Her face was no longer beautiful; her skin had turned to cellophane and I could almost see the plastic bones crackling beneath. That night I could not describe the colour of the bruises she wore like gaudy jewels but now I can; until the night at the hospital, the night Aurora was born, I had never seen a person coloured so blue.

❧

The next day and night my mother did not go out. Then she became restless but, as she rarely sat still for any length of time, I did not worry too much. I thought she paced because she was cold; her skin was covered with goose bumps and she shivered throughout a day so hot that even the flies stopped moving. The following day she collapsed into bed and vomited almost without pause for another two days and told me that her bones hurt so much there would soon be nothing left of them but dust. At night her body contorted in her sleep and I wanted to tie her to the bed lest she fly away. Her screams split apart the hairs on my head, stabbed through the duvet I'd pulled over my ears and shattered the last little pieces of me that still took a teddy bear to bed.

I told myself that she had the flu, even though it was summer, that Panadol and orange juice would make her better, but she pushed the Panadol away and could not keep the juice down so in the end I sat on the floor by her bed and passed her a newly wet face washer whenever the last one dried out. She told me to leave but she was too weak to make me. Every minute that passed hammered the same thought into my mind—if this is the end, I wonder if she thinks it was worth it.

After a week the sun became lost in the clouds and the house cooled. I realised I must have fallen asleep on the floor because I woke up to the sound of a tap running. My mother was washing her face. She turned to me when she heard me move and said, 'Could you help me to have a bath?'

I nodded, stood and ran a bath, then held her hand and steadied her as she stepped in. She sat in the water with her knees hugged to her chest and her arms clasped around them, shaking. Naked, she seemed less like a wraith than she had for the last few days. The slight fold of flesh on her stomach, the loose skin on her upper arms and the gentle creasing on her chest made her both more real and more adult. My young body did not have these imperfections, would not have them until I too was older, and the contrast restored a shred of order to our relationship.

I squeezed some of her favourite bath gel onto a sponge and rubbed it across her back and down her arms. Then I scooped handfuls of water and let it run over her body, watching the bubbles burst and disappear.

'Thank you,' she said and I nodded again.

I helped her out of the bath and she managed to dry herself. I found her some clean underwear and a T-shirt and made her a plate of toast. As she sat in bed sipping water and nibbling at the toast she said to me, 'Let's go home.'

I wanted to scream and jump and shout but by then I was so tired that all I could say was, 'Yes.'

When the taxi arrived to take us to the airport, I took my mother's hand, which was resting small and loose in her lap, and pulled her gently to her feet. Her legs shook a little as they bore her weight but I slipped my arm around her waist so that she would not fall and she let me guide her into the cab and then laid her head on my shoulder and closed her eyes. She stayed like that on the plane and again on the train from Paris to Saint Pierre-des-Corps and so instead of talking I watched strange but familiar colours, trees and sky flash past, like a stream of memories unravelling too quickly for me to make any sense of them.

But when we disembarked she seemed to find herself and she put on some make-up, brushed her hair and made me find her a dress from her suitcase that was decent and ladylike and not too crushed. It took me some time but I pulled out one that she said Mémé had made for her a long time ago.

'Perfect!' she cried. 'What would I do without you Gaelle? Now, you wait there a moment and I'll go to the ladies and change and then I'll call Mémé and Pépé and tell them we're on our way.'

I sat on my suitcase and read all the signs written in the language of my childhood and I smiled at the sun and almost did not recognise my mother when she emerged. The child-woman from the photo was gone and a grown-up stood in her place.

'We'll stay overnight in Amboise. In a hotel room,' my mother announced. She jangled some keys. 'I've hired a car and we'll have one night of luxury before we go back to the farm.'

'Why can't Mémé and Pépé come and pick us up?'

'I want to surprise them. I haven't rung them yet. Imagine the looks on their faces when you walk up the road to the house. Everyone likes surprises.'

It was then that I should have paid more attention. Listened to the flicker of a question in my mind: when *I* walk up the road?

But I didn't ask. I nodded and thought that yes, it would be a good surprise.

As we drove into Amboise, I began to recognise landmarks, signposts of infancy and time past. There was the approach to town, oak trees arched over the road, blocking out the sky, as if the branches were the supports of heaven. The gentleness of light sieved by leaves, occasionally gold but sometimes muddied by clouds. And the river, its path assured.

When we arrived at the hotel, I looked around for the luxury my mother had promised but could find nothing of the sort in the choking scent of tobacco and the shared bathroom at the end of the hall. There was a view of the river from the toilet if you stood on the bowl and I thought that, perhaps, was it: the luxury.

My mother, though, could apparently see past the smoke and shared ablutions and was floating on her back on the bed, smiling. 'Imagine, Gaelle! Nothing to do tonight except spend time with you. We'll eat cheese and chocolate in bed and talk and laugh all night, like the girls and their midnight feasts in those books you read.'

And we did. Just like mother and daughter.

As she chatted about how wonderful it would be for me to be back on the farm again, she passed me thick slices of cheese and popped chocolates into my mouth and I began to relent. To believe in the story once again.

Then, when the food was finished and our eyes were tired of trying to piece images together out of the grainy black and white dots on the television, my mother turned to me with a look in her eyes that I did not recognise. I am sure now that it was fear.

'Gaelle, you're so old now. Thirteen. So grown-up. I can hardly believe it. You know that I love you, don't you?'

I nodded because I did still believe it. I could count on one hand the number of times she had said those words to me but I told myself it made them all the more precious. Of course, there was not any hidden meaning in her frugality; she was perfectly happy, most of the time, loving only herself.

'You're nearly too old for stories, aren't you?' she continued.

I considered. Possibly I was, but the stories were pieces of my mother, something to hold on to.

'No, not quite too old,' she said. 'And this story starts to get very grown-up. Desdemona's story.' As she spoke, I could feel her words draw around us like a blanket, binding us together.

'I know where we are up to, Gaelle. I thought about it on the train. Desdemona is pregnant and she is about to tell Hero but they hear the voices of the people in the kingdom coming after them. That's right, isn't it?'

I nodded and laid my head on the pillow beside her.

'Well, Hero looks at Desdemona for a moment, making a promise with his eyes that will not be kept. They begin to run. Houses flash past them and Desdemona sees glimpses through windows of the mothers and children contained within every home. Some are embracing, some are shouting, some are laughing, some are playing; others are sitting in chairs with vacant stares as if their energy has fallen out of their eyes, like tears, and been wiped away.

'Desdemona puts her hand to her stomach and shouts, *We can't keep running, they have horses; they are too fast.*

'Hero circles around. *Back to the cave*, he calls and they return to their home. He digs a tunnel beneath the cave, deep into the ground, and he tells her to stay there, buried in the womb of the earth where no one will ever find her.

'She asks, W*hat about you?* and he replies, *I'll come back to find you. I'll kill everybody and then I will come.*

'The girl slips into the tunnel and waits, not noticing the days and weeks pass by because she is so enraptured with the stories she is told by her wings and her horn and her own ability to conjure up all kinds of possibilities for the missing parts. But one day, mid-story, she feels her stomach contract. She shifts position but it happens again. And she understands that this is the moment. The baby is coming. The next pain she feels is a familiar shock of love. The contract between her and the child. A contract that can never be broken; she will always be a mother and this will always be her child. She is forever tied, she wants to be tied because she knows it is an attachment of the most intimate kind but it is also the most terrifying.

'Then one of her wings begins to fissure, to fall away like aged paper. And with each pain across her stomach, pieces of her other wing crumble. *No,* she shouts as the story breaks up. She stops thinking about the child. She stops thinking about the pains. She wishes them away. It works for a few minutes: no more pain and her remaining wing ceases to shed its skin.

'She remembers the houses that she and Hero saw when they were running away. Every house had a mother, every house had children. She did not see a woman without a child. And she knows that this has always been the snake's intention. That she will regain her humanity by becoming a mother. Because that is what a woman is supposed to do. But she will also understand the horror of motherhood and the beauty and the loss. She will have to give up the stories. She will lose the pieces of herself that she most wants to keep.

'So what does Desdemona do faced with that kind of choice? Humanity versus story. Fantasy versus the child. Fantasy is so alluring but sometimes the best thing for you is just an embrace from your daughter.'

My mother lay down next to me, on her side, and slipped one arm under my neck and the other over my shoulders. She gave me one of those hugs that you share with your mother when you are six years old and it is the funniest thing in the world to squeeze each other so hard that you almost cannot breathe. But this time I felt none of the happiness and only the crush and I wondered, if she held on any tighter, whether both of us would break.

TWENTY-THREE

The people milling on the lawn begin to move towards the now open doors of the exhibition. Marie comes over to collect us and Selena sighs. 'Why do we always get to the good bit and have to stop?'

As we walk towards the hall, Marie's attention is claimed by a couple with a red pram. It is the same as the pram I bought for Aurora, selected because it was rated by *Choice* magazine as the safest on the market and I did not want anything bad to happen to her in her pram, did not want her to tumble out, to suffocate; these were accidents that people—Jason's mother and sister, especially—warned me about.

Marie introduces me to the couple. Then she says, 'Can I have a cuddle?' and she leans over and smiles into the pram, arms outstretched, ready to love this bundle because it is a baby and all babies are, by definition, loveable, meant to be wrapped in cuddles.

The mother lifts the baby out of the pram, eager to show her off. She holds the baby up in the air for just a second and her husband presses his face into the baby's belly, tickling, inhaling. The baby's face sparkles, her smile is bolder than the light. Then she laughs; she is symphonic. If I could scoop that moment out of time, I would. That single but absolute instant of adoration passing between husband—wife—child.

My throat is full of all the crying I should have done a long time ago. And that is the exact moment Selena and Marie choose to turn around.

'Are you all right?' Marie asks.

'Yeah, you look...' Selena's voice trails off, unable to describe how it is that I look.

I nod my head. 'Let's go inside.'

Selena leads the way into a room that is full, too full, of people pointing and staring and examining images. My eyes search but the four walls of the room yield nothing. Just row after row of turquoise beaches, immobile, frozen into postcard perfection.

My shirt feels too tight, my make-up too stiff. I want to peel everything away.

My eyes move away from the four walls of the room to the centre. There, in the middle, spotlit, crowded, is a selection of photographs. A feature. A centrepiece. An attraction. I push past people. Stop. Stare.

There is the dawn light. There is the girl floating like a ghost, flying like a unicorn, swimming like a mermaid, through the light. And the girl again, spinning by a bonfire with braided hair. And here she is, suspended against the night, haloed by the moon; she is a goddess, a star, a fleeting comet. Now she is lit by water droplets, arms outstretched, embracing, perhaps, or waving goodbye. Then the last image. Her smiling head.

Artefacts. Memories. Stories. The box is open. Selena has set everything free.

I turn and see another picture. I am in the photo with her. Selena's face is not visible; it is clear only that she is a child. I am standing behind her, in the shadows, and it is not because I am gazing romantically, Madonna-like, at her, it is just because the tradition of such images of a woman and a child is so established it needs no explanation. In the photograph I am a mother.

I begin to back away but the images seem to chase me, like Pandora's sins. I start to run and people stare—or do they?—perhaps I am making that up too.

The exhibition is near the beach, as everything is down here, but it is the wrong beach, not mine. Thick sand slows me down and I stumble into the water, fully clothed, shielding my eyes against the light. Water drops splash splash splash; the salt of my eyes stings me or is it the sea?

It all pours out again. The steel barred bed. The nurses. The epidural. Strange faces. A screen. Green cloth. My legs, numb. Shouting. Pulling. Tearing. A baby. Jason. At the door. Sees the baby. Leaves. Doctor takes the baby. Not mine any more. Aurora.

Aurora: a baby who did not make a sound. A baby the colour of dusk. A baby who left her life inside me.

TWENTY-FOUR

'Gaelle?'

It's the softest question. I turn to Selena but am blinded by eyes that cannot seem to spill the water as fast as they fill back up again. My hand claws at the air. The girl takes it and we stand knee-deep in sea. As my eyes clear, I can see that she knows, at least part of it; that I am a liar, that I lie to others, but worst of all, that I lie to myself. This girl with the flaming hair and unremarkable eyes has seen the truth and yet she is still here, holding my hand.

ॐ

As we drove to my grandparents' farm, my mother rested one hand on the steering wheel while her other hand clasped mine. Landmarks—churches, villages, farms—passed by too slowly. At first I thought it was anticipation making time sluggish but then I realised that the route we were taking was full of loops and turns and doubling backs.

The day was warm and the wind was fresh and the light was reckless. My mother wore a scarf over her hair and told me she was Grace Kelly.

'Who am I then?' I asked.

'A princess too, of course.'

But I didn't feel like a princess. I felt the way I did that night at the farm before my mother took me away. As if things were shifting.

'Look!' I shouted, pointing at chequered fields full of goats and lupins and rapeseed. 'We're nearly there.'

My mother slowed the car and stopped at the dirt track leading to the farm.

'Why are you stopping here?' I said.

'Let's stand here a moment, together. Let's just watch.'

And so we got out of the car and she hugged me and we looked at the house in the distance, but I wanted to be inside with Mémé and Pépé rather than out there, capturing the farm in my mind as my mother was doing, commemorating something that was impossible to forget.

I pulled away.

My mother's last words to me were, 'Go, run on ahead and tell them you're here.'

And I did. I ran through the grass until I was halfway between my mother and the house and then for some reason I turned but all I could see was what looked like a unicorn standing in the spot where my mother had stood. I closed my eyes and when I opened them again there was only a horse and the clouds had drowned the sun and the only thing on the track was a girl in a green dress swimming in grass.

TWENTY-FIVE

And here is another tale of a girl in a green dress. She is at her thirtieth birthday party, a party she fled from several months ago. She is standing at the prow of a boat, staring down at her reflection in the water, fingering the dress; it is one of the few things her mother left behind and is reminiscent of seawater.

She drinks champagne with her husband. There is silence. And then she says, 'We should have brought Aurora.'

'We couldn't, Ellie.'

'Why?'

Jason took hold of my arms and held me so tightly that I ached because he could never let go. His reply was so quiet and gentle that, at the time, I could not take in his words because they were at odds with his tone. But I can hear his words now; it is almost as if he is standing beside me, and I can also hear, for the first time, the embrace in his voice that I chose not to accept as he said, 'Ellie, you can't keep pretending. She died. Inside you. When she was born.'

I had to pretend. Because I was a mother, a mother who had no child. All I knew was that the ability to tell a story can save a life. Keeping Aurora alive in my mind saved the mother that I am, but that no one else thought I was.

PART V

TWENTY-SIX

The water teases my toes and, as I look into its depths, my attention is caught by the things reflected there: my face, Selena's face, a never-ending sky. I have never noticed the reflections before. I have been too intent on the light slanting off the surface.

Selena begins to walk and my feet follow her, thinking she will, somehow, take me home. But instead she takes me back to the exhibition. I stop walking when I realise where we are going.

'It'll be all right, Gaelle,' she says and I wonder why I should believe her. But I do and I continue to follow until we are back in the room and I realise that no one except Selena and perhaps her mother has even noticed my flight and that people are only looking at me now because the bottom of my skirt is wet from seawater and is flapping about my legs.

We stand in front of my photographs. They are all of a girl floating in light, disconnected, just beyond reach. A girl with no future. Me. My mother. Aurora. And the girl with a future holding my hand.

Then there is the final image. One I had forgotten we took. Selena and I. She saw the secret in the photograph.

She has let it out. Now I see it too. She is saying goodbye. It is time to go home. This is what is left over, after.

'They're beautiful, Gaelle,' she says.

I look at them again and say, 'Yes. They are.'

TWENTY-SEVEN

'Do you have a picture of her?' Marie asks after we have returned to Siesta Park and the three of us are sitting on the chairs in front of my cottage. It is a moonless night, the black lit only by a faint glow from the highway and windows of light from the neighbouring cottages. The sea is calm this evening, we can hear only what sounds like a low breath as the water is inhaled and exhaled over and over.

I take out my phone and find the message from Jason with the photo from the hospital. 'Only this one,' I say as I pass it to her.

Selena peers over her mother's shoulder. 'Wow, she's tiny.'

I laugh. 'All babies are, Aurora's no different in that respect.'

Marie passes my phone back to me and I am so thankful that she doesn't say anything about what a beautiful baby she is or how much she looks like her mother or father. Aurora has been seen and that is enough.

'Jason loved that she was just the right size to tuck her head into the crook of his elbow and lie her body along his forearm. I'd forgotten that,' I say.

'Or just put it out of your mind for a while,' Marie replies.

'Maybe.' I nod. I hesitate only a moment before I add, 'It's nice to talk about her.'

And we do, till past midnight, not just me, but Marie and Selena too, about mothers and their daughters.

Before they leave I ask Selena to take a photo of me on my phone. The night has washed away my make-up, my hair is twisted with salt and I look tired. But after they are gone I send the photo to Jason. He sends one straight back. A photo of him, taken by him at arm's length, so the camera is almost looking down upon him. And I sit in a chair and I hug my phone and I cry some more because what I really want is to be sitting in a chair, holding him.

I go to bed later but cannot sleep. My mind is full of Jason. And Aurora. In not thinking about them, they have become caricatures in my mind, outlines: a husband, a child, rather than my husband, my child. Now I am ready to remember them as they were, define them by their presence, rather than their absence.

The first night I spoke to Jason, it was as if an act of sorcery had cast him there, through time. A blond, bronzed man-god, mouth full of winged words. It was New Year's Eve. Fireworks at the beach.

I had watched Jason for some time before that night.

He was always in the centre of a group of friends. His conversation appeared effortless. He was filled with complete assurance.

Imogen introduced us. He said my name, nothing more. 'Gaelle.'

'Jason.'

'When you speak, you sound like you're kissing your words,' he said.

'You are an accomplished flirt.'

'I think you might be too.'

The fireworks ended. The New Year began. Lovers kissed. We did not. Instead, we sat on the shore at Bondi Beach, watching the waves pushing forwards and back like lovers, compromising. A silence that was too laden with romantic expectation sat between us. So I broke it. 'Imogen said you're a doctor.'

'A heart surgeon.'

I laughed.

'Usually women are impressed by that,' Jason said. 'I suppose they think I must be loaded.'

'So why didn't you use it as your opening line?'

'Because you're studying Arts with Imogen. Arts students are all cynics.'

'Not too cynical to be sitting on a beach on New Year's Eve with a heart surgeon, though.'

This time, he laughed. And I wanted to hold that piece

of time in my hand like a photograph, linger over it. But the moment passed into its grave, or wherever it is that time goes once spent. I was left with God Fallen from Sky, Reclining on Sand or The Hero, Handsome, as heroes must be.

'So why are you doing an Arts degree?' Jason continued.

'You mean, what do I want to do? Did you always want to be a heart surgeon?'

'My dad's a surgeon. So's my brother-in-law. And you didn't answer my question.'

'I like photography. I thought I wanted to be a photographer. But I don't know why I'm studying Arts. All we do is talk about French men with too much time on their hands who've decided that everything is a sign.'

'So how did you get into photography?'

'Because of a woman who was kind to me a long time ago. And because of Kafka.'

He smiled. 'That sounds arty.'

'You mean pretentious.'

'Hey, I'm a heart surgeon. I'm the last person to call anyone pretentious. Tell me about Kafka.'

'Kafka said we photograph things in order to drive them out of our minds.' What I didn't say was that men were usually impressed by a woman who could quote Kafka off-the-cuff.

'Then I'd better make sure you never take my picture.'

And then pieces of time did sit suspended around us.

We were at the edge of a moment of before. About to move into after.

Jason called me the next day. 'Meet me at Bondi Beach,' he said.

So I chose the bikini that made the most of my too-flat chest and the caftan that fell just below my buttocks. I glossed my lips and curled my lashes. As I took his hand in mine and led him down to the water, I saw the way he looked at my legs. He had not worn a T-shirt. His body was finely worked.

We waited at the line where the water lapped the sand. The shore was patterned with shells, a scripture of sea-bones, spelling out not sentences or words, but impressions, indentations, primitive markings. Stories that are known without being told.

'I dreamed about you last night,' Jason said.

I moved my eyes away from the markings in the sand to his face. 'You're not short of opening lines, are you?'

He shook his head. 'It's not a line. I did dream about us.'

'Us? Or me?'

'Us.'

'And what were we doing, in your dream? Although I think I know what you're going to say.'

'Crying.'

'Okay, that's not what I thought you were going to say. Why were we crying?'

'I don't know. Our faces were blurry.'

'Did anything else happen?'

'It was weird. You were taking photos of my heart.'

'I thought I was the one taking classes in symbolism.'

Jason laughed. 'Yes. I like things to be a bit more tangible.'

'If our faces were blurred, how do you know it was me?'

'Because I loved you.'

We walked back to his apartment in a shadowy dusk that hinted and hid and partly revealed. Our hands were joined and people stepped around us as if sensing something not easily separated.

Jason's apartment was a study in the rectilinear: tiled floors, modular sofas and rows of shelves, most of which supported bronze sculptures of bodies and their parts. I found only one shelf that held pieces of him: medical texts, a line of photo albums labelled by year and filed in the correct order, a pile of framed certificates, placed in such a way that they were not quite on display. Awards for the highest achievement in Medicine. Cardiothoracic Surgery. Underneath, a dive ticket.

'Champagne?' Jason asked. 'I bought French. Krug.'

'Thanks.'

He handed me a glass.

'Why did you want to be a surgeon?' I asked.

He shrugged. 'To save lives.'

'Is it really that simple?'

'I like to think it is.'

We stepped out onto the balcony. The breeze was absent. We watched the world and sipped champagne and then I turned my body to face his. I took his glass and mine and placed them on the ledge. I touched the centre of his chest with my index finger and felt him inhale. Then I traced a line along his chest, feeling the swell and dip of each hard muscle.

I think the breeze must have come in then because I shivered.

Jason stopped my hand before it reached the band of his shorts. He touched my hair, smiled and lifted off a strand of green. 'Aphrodite with seaweed baubles,' he said. Then he slipped his fingers behind my ear and undid first one earring and then the other and I could feel the touch of his flesh against mine as he stroked my lobes with his thumb and index finger.

I stepped towards him and we simply stood, so close but not quite close enough, savouring that second of anticipation, of not quite knowing. It was a feeling so fine I cannot quite believe we caught it.

And then we were kissing with the carelessness of knowing we didn't have to stop. It was a kiss like living. Or perhaps like dying.

The first time we made love, it was there, on that balcony with the scent of sea-salted air wrapped around us, my caftan still on, Jason's clothes long since gone, my back pressed to the wall, his hands supporting my thighs, his tongue tasting the skin along my neck, and my orgasm so unexpected in its quickness, its strength.

Later, while Jason slept, I left. I went to France. To see Mémé and Pépé. I thought that, by fleeing, he would see the person I really was. He would forget about the person he thought I was: *Aphrodite with seaweed baubles*.

And we could finish before we had begun.

TWENTY-EIGHT

'Why did you run away?' Jason asked as he stood on my doorstep the morning after I returned from France.

'Because I don't know how to stay.' The truth was out of my mouth before I could stop it.

We stood silently for a few moments on either side of the doorway, Jason's skin coloured rose by light passing through plum leaves, hair fashionably disordered, face hurt, unsmiling. 'Normally, if someone wanted to run away, I'd let them,' he said.

'Why did you come to find me?'

He folded his arms and turned around. Shook his head. 'Because ... I missed you. I tried not to.'

I remembered how gently he'd removed my earrings that night at Bondi, remembered the moment of being not quite close enough and then I remembered the kiss that followed. 'I missed you too.'

I could see him trying not to smile. Then he turned back to face me. My betraying hand lifted like the arm of a marionette to touch his cheek.

'Gaelle, come with me to Palm Beach for the weekend. We can use my parents' weekender. Just get changed and come. You don't need to bring anything.'

Yes, I thought. I will come and I will leave everything else behind.

The next day we spread out a blanket on the beach; we were alone because the grey clouds were keeping less romantic souls indoors. Jason poured champagne and opened a basket full of bread and pâté and fruit that he had gone out to buy in the morning while I slept.

'You know, you defy logic,' I said.

He sipped champagne and fed bread to me like lovers do. 'What do you mean?'

'You don't give up, give in, see anything else in me but a girl you think you love.'

'I think I see more of you than you want to show, Gaelle.'

Raindrops began to drizzle from the sky.

'You think you've worked me out.'

'No, I don't.'

At that moment, the drizzle became a solid wall of water; it caused the bread to disintegrate and the glasses to fill. Jason pulled me up, laughing, and we ran back to the car, leaving everything right there on the sand.

We curled up together in the back of his four-wheel drive, rubbing away the fog from the windows, watching the storm break over the sea, clothes plastered to our skin, not caring.

He brushed wet hair off my face. 'Do you have any family here?'

'My mother's dead. I don't remember her.'

Half-truths. But he believed me.

As the storm began to lift, Jason leaned in to kiss me, opening my mouth to his, shifting his leg against mine, and with it, shifting desire from something that can be written down, remembered and relived to something almost too intense to bear.

I thought then that I was ready to stop running.

We bought our house one month before the wedding but did not move in until we came back from our honeymoon. Jason wanted a terrace in Woollahra. I wanted a house with age and worn edges, wooden floors I could polish, fireplaces I could tile and a kitchen I could fill with Mémé's copper pots and the smell of Pépé's goats cheese. I was surprised when we found a house that fit all our criteria. Jason was not.

'See, Gaelle,' he said. 'It's meant to be.' He took my hand and led me from room to room, showing me where the fireplaces were, the hooks in the kitchen that were made for hanging pots, and the room that was the perfect size for a nursery.

'Three years,' he said. 'We'll be ready to fill this room in three years. Imagine a beautiful baby girl who'll look just like you.'

'It might make a good darkroom,' I said.

He laughed. 'I don't know. Do you think there's enough room in the house for a darkroom? And where would the baby go?'

'We don't have a baby yet.'

'There's no point fitting it out as a darkroom and then redoing it all as a nursery in three years time.'

'But photography's important to me.'

Jason hugged me and said, 'I know it is. And it will still be important even if we don't have a darkroom.'

'I've always wanted one.'

'We don't need to decide now. We want the house anyway.'

I realised then that we had been too busy falling in love to talk about babies and dreams and whether I would always be a beauty editor and I also realised that, even if we did talk about those things, I did not know what I would say. I was not well-taught when it came to thinking about the future and now it was happening before I had decided whether or not I wanted it.

From then on, Jason called the room the nursery. I called it the spare room. And then, Aurora's room.

I dressed for the wedding in the spare room, surrounded by unpacked boxes and unplaced furniture. Mémé helped me while Pépé flirted with Imogen because she was the only person, outside family, who could understand him.

I smiled at Mémé and she kissed my cheeks. 'We're so proud of you, Gaelle.'

And that was all it took to transform me into a six-year-old girl with tears on her cheeks, folding herself into her grandmother's arms.

'She would be proud of you too, Gaelle. And she would like Jason.'

'Yes, she would.' He was a man, after all.

'You've told him about her, haven't you, *chérie*?'

I nodded. Another half-truth.

'I want Jason and me to be like you and Pépé,' I whispered. 'In love forever. A family.'

Mémé kissed my forehead. Then we turned to my reflection in the mirror. I don't think either of us saw the details—a scooped neck and high waist. Instead we saw a legacy, the familial bond between us as solid as the earth on the farm, passed on through her wedding dress—now mine—to me.

For the rest of the day, I was afraid of tearing the fabric and ruining the image forever.

Outside the church, Pépé straightened my veil. 'You look so much like…' He cleared his throat. 'Lili. And your grandmother,' he finished. 'I wanted to bring you a goat for your present, Gaelle. But quarantine …'

We laughed and the lines on his face formed a calligraphy of love.

'We will send you the kitchen table. It is a table that should be used by a family.'

'Thank you, Pépé.'

We turned to face the open doors. I reminded myself that Mémé and Pépé had survived my mother. So would I.

When we went to visit the photographer to select pictures for the wedding album, we had our first fight. We swept into the studio holding hands, sunburnt after our honeymoon, full of our newlywed status and sat down in front of a pile of photographs. The first was taken through the front doors of the church, up the aisle, as Pépé and I walked towards the altar. We are backlit and this makes it difficult to see Jason clearly in the darkness by the altar. I put the photograph on the yes pile.

'Not that one,' he said. 'You can't see anyone's face.'

'But that's what I like about it. It's like a picture from a book. The blurry groom. The unrevealed bride.'

He laughed. 'Gaelle, people want to see faces. Not backs and dark patches.'

'I wasn't thinking about other people. I was thinking about us.'

'But the album's as much for our friends and family as it is for us.'

I passed him the pile of photographs. 'Which do you like then?'

'Well if you want it to be like a picture book, maybe it could tell a story. Let's start at the church and show the main things there, like the vows and the kiss, and then move to the reception and do the speeches, the cake and the dance.'

I realised that for him, a story was about chronology whereas what I had meant was to capture impressions, a feeling, a sense of us. But before I could reply, he said, 'We could start with this one.'

It was a photograph of me, stepping up to the altar. Spears of light thrown down by stained glass windows are making kaleidoscopic patterns on my dress. I look as though I am reaching out to touch the colours but they are slipping through my fingers.

'You look gorgeous, Gaelle. Sort of overwhelmed.'

'But you're not in it.'

Jason put the photograph on the yes pile.

'And here's a great one of Mum and Dad,' he said.

I laughed. 'Yes, it is a good one.'

Margaret's head is bowed. She is praying, most likely, that I might turn out to be a good wife and a good mother.

'Then I'd like this one of Mémé and Pépé.'

Jason glanced at it. 'They look a bit serious, Gaelle. Isn't there a better one?'

In response, I added the photograph to the yes pile. Jason shrugged.

He passed me another photograph. Jason and Gaelle. Beneath the sacred heart of Jesus. She becomes his.

I shook my head. 'Not that one.'

'But that's my favourite.'

'Why?'

'We look happy. In love.'

'I don't think we do.'

Jason said, 'But we are in love. How else would we look?'

'We won't always look like we're in love. Like now, for instance. We look like we're fighting.'

'We're not fighting.'

'What are we doing then?' I asked.

'We're not fighting about wedding photos.'

'We are.'

'We're deciding.'

'We're disagreeing.'

'We're allowed to do that, you know,' Jason said. 'It doesn't mean it's a fight.'

I picked up the next photo. The finale. The couple walking down the aisle, arm in arm, bound together. I discarded it and moved to the next one. The congregation, mouths wide open, singing a hymn whose words were supposed to remind us that a church was a place where miracles occurred.

TWENTY-NINE

After we were married we often spent weekends cycling along the northern beaches, stopping beneath the open sun to picnic, to kiss, to laugh. And some afternoons, when Jason returned from scuba diving, mind and body quiet for once, we sat on the front verandah in the lingering dusk with a bottle of champagne and he told me about the life that passed beneath the water and we ate a mound of cold prawns straight out of the shell and then later, we kissed over cognac and it was like that first night on the balcony all over again and there was only his body, my body, our bodies, us.

The demands of Jason's work made it difficult to catch up with friends, and I often found myself at Imogen's house on a Saturday night having dinner with her and her family. Then Jason instigated the great dinner party plan so that he could see all of his friends at once by having everyone over to our house for dinner every third Friday, strictly scheduled so he could be sure of being there.

That was a time of efflorescence; everything around us seemed to swell and bloom into full, wet fertility. We were surrounded by mothers, or mothers-to-be. And then, apparently, it was my turn.

On this particular Friday night I cooked platters of asparagus crumbled with goats cheese, potatoes fried in goose fat, duck confit. When it was time to eat, I sat with Imogen and Rehana.

'When do you hear about the promotion?' I asked Rehana.

She sighed. 'I think they're stalling. Maybe they're going to look outside the company for someone but they don't want to tell me yet.'

'Why?' Imogen asked.

'You know what it's like. In a company full of women, only the men seem to be senior management material.'

'But your sales manager's female, isn't she? ' I said.

'The token one. So they don't need another.'

'They're just scared that the women are going to run off and have babies,' Imogen added.

Rehana laughed. 'Well they do. You did.'

Imogen laughed too. 'I know. Blame it all on me. But I went back.'

'Besides,' I said, 'I can't imagine you running off anywhere to have babies.'

'No,' she said. 'I can't either.'

Somehow the group of mothers sitting in the middle of the table had heard the word babies and then it began.

Melanie led with the poo story. 'You wouldn't believe what Gracie did today,' she said. 'She did a poo in her nappy then took it off and hid it in the playroom and wouldn't tell me where it was. I could smell it all morning but do you think I could find it? Turned out she'd put it in the Play-Doh tub because she thought it might be fun to make animal shapes out of it.'

Then Geraldine opened the competitive comparisons. 'Olivia's just stopped wearing a nappy to bed. It's so nice not to have to clean up bottoms any more, at least for another month or so.' She patted her stomach which looked to me as if it contained an elephant calf rather than a human baby and I wondered if I should put a mat under her chair so that her waters didn't break all over my antique rug.

But the conversation quickly moved on to a new level when Geraldine leaned over to give Tracy, who had just had her first child, a spreadsheet. 'It's got all the different size packs and the regular price of each. Then I've listed the best sale price I've ever found for each pack size. So when you're checking the catalogues, you know whether it's worth going out to stock up with four or five boxes because it's a really good special or whether you should just get one of the smaller packs to tide you over until you can get them cheaper.'

'Thanks Gerry, that's great,' Tracy replied, putting the paper into her new luggage-sized handbag that would surely hold at least a year's supply of baby wipes.

Imogen, noticing the look of confusion on my face, whispered in my ear, 'It's the famous nappy spreadsheet. We all got a copy when we had a baby.'

I laughed, at first because I didn't believe her and then because I did. But as I watched Geraldine dispensing more advice about shitting and sleeping and eating and recalled the articles she'd written on food shortages and coral bleaching and severe weather events, I wondered if it was as banal to her as it was to me and if the only way she had to escape it was to make spreadsheets about nappies.

I said loudly, to Rehana and Imogen, hoping everyone would hear and divert the flow of conversation, 'Are you having any holidays this year? Jason wants to go to France and see Mémé and Pépé because he hasn't seen them since the wedding but I was thinking about spa holidays in the Maldives.'

'Sounds like heaven,' Imogen replied. 'We might go skiing, give the kids their first go on the slopes.'

I smiled. 'I'll buy Zahra some après-ski boots for Christmas.'

'God, she'd love that. And you can probably get them for two year olds these days.'

Melanie interrupted. 'They make everything for kids now. I saw a baby with a Pandora bracelet the other day. But you'll need to get your spa holiday in quick, Gaelle, because you won't be able to do stuff like that when you've got kids. It must be your turn. I'm not going to do it again, at least not for a while.'

As if motherhood was a merry-go-round whose spinning force would eventually pull every one of us into its ride of toy ponies and tinny lullabies. 'I don't think I'm in the line,' I replied.

Melanie frowned, unsure if I was joking or just being French and I turned to the male end of the table in search of more diverting conversation.

What I heard, from Tony, was this, directed at Jason: 'Nah, today's rally was a dead cat bounce. Buy tomorrow. It'll be cheaper.' And Gus's reply, 'No matter what you do, Jase, it'll go down by a couple of bucks the minute you buy it. Least that's what always happens to me.'

Later, when everyone had gone and I was standing in the kitchen with Jason, washing the dishes, he kissed my hair and asked, 'Did they do it again?'

'Yes,' I sighed. 'Thank God Imogen and Rehana came. At least they can talk about something other than the technicalities of nappy prices.'

He wrapped his arms around me from behind while I washed mismatched antique china. 'Ellie,' he said, 'we always said we'd wait three years, and it's been longer than that now. You won't lose your personality just because you have a baby. There isn't a devil in the delivery suite making you trade one for the other.'

Jason spun me around, peeled off my rubber gloves and smiled, his charming assurance still in place after all this time.

'That's not what I'm worried about,' I said.

'What then?'

I shifted, wanting to turn around, but I was caught in his arms. 'It's just … the whole idea of being a mother. It's not that I don't want a child. But I'm not so sure I want to be a mother.'

Jason laughed. 'It's hard to have one without the other.'

'But what would we do with it? No, what would *I* do with it? Because I'd be the one looking after it and how do I do that and still do everything else?'

'You know you don't have to work after we have a baby but I know you'll get bored if you don't. So we'll get a nanny or something.'

'I'm not having a baby and then palming it off to someone else to look after. If you have a child, you're meant to look after it.'

'You could work part-time, do both, that's not palming it off.'

'What, and do a half-arsed job of each? Besides, it's not like that's all there is to do. If I had any spare time, I'd like to do more photography.'

'You haven't been doing much of that lately.'

'Because there's too much other stuff on. I'm always stuck in the kitchen cooking for dinner parties while you're at work till the middle of the night.'

'Ellie, what's going on? You love cooking and you know I have to work long hours. How did we get from having a baby to the time I spend at work?'

Cool night air flooded through the open window, lifting the curtain so it billowed like a ghost. I shivered. I hadn't heard from my mother in fifteen years. But it was as if she'd slipped in with the draught to remind me of what she had bequeathed to me: my unshakeable belief that to really love a child meant to be with it every moment, to never leave, to be always together. I did not know how I could do that, just as I did not know how to let my mother be dead.

And then Jason filled in the silence with his own belief. 'Besides, you'd be a great mother.'

'How do you know?'

'Because I love you.'

He kissed my lips and sealed our fate with the way he always knew what to say.

I rested my head against Jason's shoulder. Such a simple act. Hands pressed to bodies. Clothes made invisible. Eyes speaking words that mouths made clumsy. Jason leading me to the bedroom, laying me down as if I was something precious, taking my foot into his hand, kissing my toes, trailing his fingers along my calf and along my thigh and then into me. Love-making. Life-making.

'Jason thinks it's time we had a baby,' I said to Imogen at work the next day.

She looked up from the glow-in-the dark nail polish she was painting onto her fingers. 'Revolting, isn't it?' She wafted her hand at me. 'My readers will love it. What did you say?'

'That I wasn't sure.'

'Did you tell him why?'

'No.'

'Gaelle, you're nothing like your mother. And Jason would understand if you told him about her. You should, you know, especially if you do decide to have a baby.'

'It's too late. I should have told him when I met him, but his family is so normal. What would they know about people like her?'

'You used to say that the one thing you wanted was to have a family of your own, like you never had. What's changed?'

'But I meant Jason and me. We're a family. I have what I want. A baby might mess things up.'

Imogen laughed. 'Well it'll definitely do that. Especially on your floor.'

I smiled. 'You know what I mean.'

'You spend enough time at my place with Zahra and Jack to know that it's more about things changing than things being messed up.'

'I suppose. And maybe if I had a baby and did everything right then I'd break the curse.'

'You're not cursed.'

'I hope I'm not.'

Friday night. Jason was at work. I'd been to Imogen's for dinner the night before and wasn't sure I could withstand another onslaught of her children's spaghetti-smeared fingers. Rehana was having a dirty weekend with her latest fling.

I went for a walk at about six o'clock, home early because I'd been at a lipstick launch where the cocktails had come to a premature end. It was the kind of evening that made you feel as if the day would never end. The sun still shone hot and bright and people were everywhere, walking, shopping, eating, laughing. I passed a couple with a baby in a pram; at the café on the corner two couples and their children were enjoying an early dinner and further on a little girl ran along the footpath with a pinwheel in her hand, giggling as it spun around and around. The children looked happy. The parents looked happy.

But I knew it wasn't that simple. Geraldine had confessed that she and Gus didn't even remember their wedding anniversary this year, let alone go out for dinner or have sex on the day. That they hadn't had sex for months. I knew from Imogen that she and Alex sometimes went for days without a kiss or a hug because they forgot, yet they always remembered to smother the children with hugs and kisses when they got home from work. And Melanie said she loved her children more than her husband. I could see from the looks on their faces that Geraldine and Imogen thought the same, that it was a kind of surrender, not something they chose, but something that happened.

I could not imagine something so powerful that it could shift the only steadiness I had ever found.

I walked back home and called Jason at work, which was something I never did. They tracked him down and he took the call; the first thing he said was, 'What's wrong, I'm about to go into theatre.'

'What if we didn't have a baby?' It was not that I'd decided, it was just that I wanted to know his answer to the question.

'Can we talk about this when I'm home? I've got a guy on a table whose chest is literally being opened up right now.'

'I'll be asleep when you get home.'

'We'll talk about it at breakfast then.'

'In the five seconds it takes you to drink your coffee and run out the door?'

Jason sighed. 'Okay. We'd feel like we were missing some-thing. We never regret the things we do Ellie, just the stuff we don't do. I've gotta go, I'm being paged.'

Then he was gone. I sat in the chair beside the phone and thought about what he had said. I hoped there was one person out there who regretted the things she had done. But did I? And, more importantly, would I, like Jason had said, regret the things I didn't do because of her? For the second time since I had met Jason I thought that it was time to stop running.

Then came *that* Father's Day. We should have taken heed then, understood we were not going to get what we wanted. Understood that things didn't always work out.

It started well enough. I let Jason sleep in until nine

o'clock because he hadn't finished at the hospital until two in the morning. I made croissants and bought his favourite jam because he couldn't get used to croissants dipped in coffee or chocolate. I made espresso and carried it all upstairs on a tray with a present. Jason opened his eyes and smiled at me as I leaned over to kiss him.

'What's this for?' He looked from the tray to my face.

'Father's Day. I thought that if we celebrated it, we might have more luck.'

'Maybe tomorrow could be Father's Day too.'

I laughed and slipped into bed beside him, curling my head into the hollow space above his heart.

He opened his present and turned it over in his hands as if he wasn't quite sure what it was.

'It's an underwater camera,' I said. 'You haven't added any-thing to your albums for years because I always end up taking the photos. I thought you could put in some pictures from your dives.'

'Thanks.' Jason leaned over and kissed me.

As he pulled away I said, 'You know, today's the day.'

He thought for a moment. 'It is, isn't it? Eat first or sex first?'

'Eat first.'

And that was how sex became an assignment, no longer about the moment itself but about the result.

Croissants and coffee consumed, we arranged ourselves, Jason above, me below. Position was now all about depth of penetration, not about pleasure. Orgasm was, for him, about the physical properties of ejaculation, not about stars exploding and worlds colliding. For me, it was simply a waste of energy. And timing was dictated by charts and thermometers and blood tests. Every second day was best. So that's what we were doing. For the stipulated time. Twelve months.

Afterwards, Jason leaned on his elbow and said, 'I always thought that sex like this would be ... I don't know ... something I wouldn't get into. You know, not being spontaneous. But if I'm holding you and kissing you and loving you, it doesn't matter. And if it has to be like this for a while, I don't care.'

How I loved him for saying that.

The next day I had an appointment with the reproductive endocrinologist.

'My cycles are irregular,' I said. 'They can be anywhere from fifty to seventy days long. I've been taking my temperature, checking my mucous, and having sex every second day. It's been twelve months. We're not pregnant. I'd like to move things along.'

'We'll need to do some tests. Find out what's wrong,' the doctor said.

I was glad that Jason was not there to hear that I was defective.

'I'll just take down some family history,' he said.

I stared at him for too long.

'Medical details of your parents. Let's start with your mother. Heart disease? Genetic disorders?'

All I had to offer him were silences, uncertainties, gaps. 'She had no physical or mental conditions,' I said.

THIRTY

Jason was the one who checked the dates. I'd suspected for a few days but hadn't said anything because when he turned to me with a look of such barely masked hopefulness, I would have done anything in my power not to wipe it away.

'I'll run to the chemist,' he said. 'Get the test.'

'I have one here.'

'Then what are we waiting for?' He laughed and leaped over to the bathroom door.

I didn't move.

'Ellie, what is it?'

'What if it's negative? Again.'

'It'll be all right. We'll just try again. More Clomid. More sex. It's not hard to take, you know.'

But I didn't think it would be all right. Not this time. I went into the bathroom. Took out the white plastic tube. Peed. Waited.

Jason tapped on the door. 'Ellie?'

'It's positive.'

His laugh was of the kind of absolute happiness that is as rare as happy endings.

'I'll do the second one. Just to make sure,' I said.

I peed again. Waited.

He tried the door handle. 'What does it say?'

'The same thing.'

'Ellie, you have to let me in. I want to hug you and kiss you. Watch you smile.'

'Can you go and buy another test?'

'Why?'

'I want to be absolutely sure.'

'Two tests are enough.'

'Not for me.'

I stood at the bathroom window and watched Jason run all the way to the chemist at the end of the street and all the way home again.

When he returned I held out my hand from behind the door. He passed me a white paper bag. Two more tests. Both positive.

I opened the door and walked straight into a wall of love. I started to cry.

Jason wiped my eyes with the pads of his fingers. 'You are happy, aren't you?'

Yes, I wanted to say.

Margaret organised a party for us. 'A baby shower that everyone can come to, not just girls,' she said, and I wondered whether she would find invitations for a Conception Party amidst those for engagements and weddings.

The night of the party, I stood in our living room because, somehow, the party ended up being held at our house, which meant I would be left with the cleaning up. I was surrounded by crimson balloons floating in bunches under lights, render-ing everything rose-coloured. Champagne glasses frothed and bubbled in everyone's hands except my own.

Jason smiled at me from across the room. Raised his glass. I smiled back, then turned to Imogen.

'I was starting to wonder if not falling pregnant was a sign that I wasn't meant to have a baby,' I said.

Imogen hugged me. 'It definitely wasn't a sign and you are pregnant so you don't have to think about it any more. I hope our kids are best friends too.'

'Of course they will be. I'll have a girl and she'll grow up to marry Jack and then we really will be family.'

Imogen laughed. 'I'm so excited for you. I hope it's a girl; I can see you with a baby girl.'

'Me too.' I smiled at Imogen and then it almost felt as though we were back on the playing fields in London. 'We're never going to move house, Im. We'll stay here forever: me, Jason and the baby. We'll visit Mémé and Pépé once a year and she'll love them as much as I do and I'll help her with her homework and I'll tell her the truth, always.'

Imogen's reply was something she would repeat to me a year later in my kitchen and I believed her the first time but not the second. 'It'll be all right, Gaelle.'

Then her attention was claimed by her husband and I went into the kitchen to refill plates of food. Margaret, damn her, saw me there, wiping my eyes when I should have been heating trays of hors d'oeuvres.

'Stop crying,' she said. 'It's a gift from God. After all this time. You've been blessed.'

'Yes,' I said, rubbing my belly and giving her the smile she was looking for. 'After all this time.'

She patted my stomach as if it were a thing with a life of its own. 'You'll feel better soon. The first few months are always the hardest. But then you'll be a mother. That's all you'll need.'

Over the next few days I felt Aurora begin with the merest flutter. But it couldn't have been, in reality, or so Jason said, because she was not yet big enough to move. How was it, then, that I could feel her thoughts, like the outstretched wings of a butterfly, rippling along the insides of my stomach, tickling me, teasing me, tempting me to love her?

The first time we saw her, she was in blurred black and white on the screen in the obstetrician's room. A tiny, alien creature with a head so large it bespoke wisdom.

'Look, it moved its hand,' Jason said as he watched.

'The baby is waving to us,' I said.

Jason turned to me and I knew how my face must also look.

'She's real now, isn't she?' I said. 'The baby. Alive.'

And he said, 'Yes.'

At our next dinner party, I found myself at the centre of the table, surrounded by motherhood, which had, it seemed, now shrouded me in its inclusive veil. Rehana sat at the end of the table, where I used to sit, in the area reserved for the non-mothers, a state of being for which I suddenly realised there was no word.

The first question came from Melanie. 'What have you bought for the baby?'

'Nothing,' I replied. 'I don't have time to shop. I'm really busy at work at the moment and I've got months to go.'

'You must have bought a book,' she said.

'A book?'

'You know, *Baby Love, Up the Duff, What to Expect When You're Expecting,* one of those.'

I shrugged and said, 'Why would I need a book? I've got you guys to tell me all I need to know.'

And then, as if I had been serious, she responded with, 'Pelvic floors, Gaelle. Do your exercises or all sorts of things can go wrong.'

'A baby monitor,' said Geraldine. 'Before I had the baby, I said I'd never get one but how else do you go outside for fifteen minutes and hang up the washing when the baby's asleep? Then you know what baby's up to all the time.'

I grinned at Imogen. 'Do I want to know?'

She laughed. 'Probably not.'

But Melanie was back to the instruction manual.

'A birth plan. Write one out and give it to your obstetrician. I did and everything went just to plan.'

After that, my life became a succession of weeks.

Fourteen weeks. Nausea stopped. I'd managed to only vomit in the bin at work once.

Eighteen weeks. I really did feel the baby move.

Twenty weeks. Jason felt the baby move too.

Twenty-one weeks. Anatomy scan. Baby was perfect. And a girl.

Twenty-eight weeks. I cried.

I came home from work after having stopped to buy groceries. I told myself that it was just twenty more steps until I could sit down. But I lied. It was more like fifty steps from the car to the kitchen.

I dropped the bags on the kitchen bench, searching for the bottle of paraffin oil laxative. I poured out forty millilitres, sipped and gagged and wondered how it was that every other pregnant woman I saw looked rosy and Rubenesque and not at all constipated, crippled and heartburnt.

The bags of pineapples, oranges, watermelon and all the other succulent fruits I craved to have dripping into my mouth were shoved unpacked in the fridge. Then I felt it again. The dizziness. I took another iron tablet, reluctantly, because it would only make the constipation worse, but the baby had exhausted my iron stores and left nothing for me.

I crumpled into the sofa. Waited for the dizziness to

pass and then saw a note from Jason on the floor, blown away because he had left it on the coffee table in the path of the draft from the front door. *Gus called. We're going diving. Back around 10pm.* I picked up the note and put it on the table. It blew onto the floor again. I leaned my head forward, resting it on my knees, remembering what the midwife had said to do about dizzy spells. I knew then why it was called a spell; I was truly overcome.

As I sat with my head in my hands, my ankles came into view and I felt as though I was looking at someone else's legs. Who belonged to the swollen flesh that was occupying the place where only this morning my ankles were located? My lower back twinged as I straightened up and again I felt that the body I was inhabiting was not my own. The tears started to fall and it was more than I could do to lift up my hand and wipe them away. Mascara pooled black under my eyes and my nose dripped. The baby kicked. I did not rub my stomach or acknowledge her communication. The baby kicked again but all I could do was cry because it was the first time she had wanted more from me than I could give.

Every week of my third trimester I walked down Queen Street. I felt that our house was too empty, too austere, when it should be filled to bursting like I was. I scoured antique shops, pressed for time, knowing that the baby would not, of course, notice the details when she came. But I hoped the treasures I found would somehow seep their history into my home and that the baby would feel this, would feel embraced, located, loved.

After one such hunt I returned home with a French ormolu clock which I placed on the dresser, noting the warmth spread by its gold facade onto the wood below. I felt then that my home was becoming a place to run your hands over, to pick up, to touch, to never put down.

'We'll wind this clock every morning my darling and then we will know that the sun has risen and the day has begun and we will talk and laugh and play until your daddy comes home to read you a story and put you to bed.' I placed my hands on my stomach. 'Then one day this clock will be yours and you will wind it in the mornings with your own baby girl and you might, from time to time, think of me and the things I have passed on to you.'

I stepped back and smiled. 'Everything is perfect now.'

Then I took out the key, wound the clock, set the hands and tapped the pendulum into motion. The clock chimed twice. Two o'clock. Play time. And I felt the baby stretch, saw the side of my stomach protrude as her feet hit the walls of my womb and I laughed as she pressed her back against my hands.

I rubbed the place where I felt the lifting flesh and she pushed into me harder. I watched the hands of the clock move as I stood without speaking in the home of my family and stroked my baby's back through a membrane of skin. And then I understood that the room was not quite finished. The walls should be lined with faces. The faces of my family.

I stole the details I wanted, re-shot them from old photographs.

Pépé's hand pressed against his cheek: the split nails and soiled flesh connected me to a familial earth. Mémé's eyes: ageless; they had moved beyond words to another kind of language. Jason's left breast: the home of his heart, pounding always with a steady expression I thought I understood. Margaret's mouth: thin, cracked; it spoke even when frozen on film. Not my mother. Me: my reflection, not my belly because that felt like not-me, but my feet on the polished wood floor, grounded, fixed, solid.

THIRTY-ONE

The hospital. Aurora's birth day. Jason. Me. Her. Sitting on the bed. A family. That was how it was supposed to be.

It was not supposed to be Jason and me looking down at the bundle in my arms as if we had seen a horror that left us without language. It was not supposed to be Jason and me, eyes, limbs, bodies, fixed and immobile, as if, through absolute stillness, we might hear one tiny breath. As if we could somehow will life into the blood-blue baby wrapped in a blanket.

'Keep her with you for a day or so,' the midwife had said. 'It'll help. Cuddle her. Talk to her. You might like to give her a name. Take some time to say goodbye.'

And then she left us in the room with pamphlets about grief and a dead baby who was, to me, like a blindness, because she was not an image, not a story, not a word.

Jason was the first to kiss her forehead. All I could do was stare like a camera trained and never shot. And then Jason began to cry, tears such as I'd never seen because Jason didn't cry, not ever; he knew how to fix everything.

Not like me. A mother who did not, could not, protect her child. If only I'd gone to the hospital earlier. Been more insistent with the midwives. Talked to her more. Played with her more. Held on tighter, harder, longer. Instead I'd let go. An instinctive action, an inherited action, something etched into my bones. If only I'd known how to be more like a mother. Then it wouldn't have happened.

'There was nothing you could have done,' the doctor said. So did the midwives. And Jason. But I did not believe them.

Because, if it was not my fault, why did the other mothers in the hospital—the ones with their crying babies—avoid me as if I was cursed? They didn't stop me in the hall to ask how my stitches were healing, to find out how I was feeling and when I was going home. And why were there classes about how to settle the baby, how to bath the baby, how to feed the baby—but nothing for mothers whose babies could not be bathed, could not be fed, could not be roused?

People sent cards. Sympathy cards. Condolences. Cards that talked obliquely about *our loss*, as if I'd misplaced a purse. I threw them in the bin. 'Perhaps we should keep those,' Jason said. 'So we can send thank you cards.'

'I don't want them,' I said. 'Those are cards for death.'

'But ...' he started to say. He could not say it.

Mémé and Pépé sent a card that said, *Congratulations. A Baby Girl*. Margaret wanted to throw that one in the bin. 'It's not appropriate,' she whispered to Jason.

I took it from her. 'This is a card for a birth,' I said. 'I gave birth. To Aurora.' Mémé and Pépé understood. I was a mother. Aurora was a baby. Not a thing that never existed.

Only a handful of people came to visit. Margaret. Penelope, Jason's sister. Because they had to. Penelope had her children with her. *I didn't know the baby would be in the room.* Margaret took them away. But not before they asked: *Why is the baby that colour?* Children always ask the right questions. But the only answer was silence.

Nobody asked to pick up Aurora, to hold her, even though that is always the first thing people ask when they visit a baby in the hospital. I'd held their babies. They could barely look at mine.

Except Imogen. She walked straight over to Aurora, cradled her and said, smiling, 'She's beautiful.'

I heard Penelope gasp as if she could not conceive of it being true. But it was. She was. Beautiful. And so was Jason. The way he held her after everybody had gone. The way he showed me her toes, her fingers, the swollen thumb that she must have sucked while she was inside my womb. The way he held me as if I too were a child. The way he tried to fix it. But he couldn't.

Then we gave her a bath. We washed away the dry skin from between her toes, along her forehead and over her knuckles. Her eyes were blue, like Jason's. Her hair was brown like mine. We dressed her in a tiny pink gown.

We hugged her for the last time before they came to take her away. I held on to her with all my strength but it wasn't enough. She was pulled away from me for the second time. For the last time.

Jason kissed her cheek and said goodbye. I did not. Because if I did not say it then she would not leave. I wanted, not just to cry, but to sob, to howl, but I knew that if I started, I would become like Niobe, fixed weeping until the end of time. Instead, I did what I could to hold the pieces of me together.

THIRTY-TWO

Consequence. Something I have never thought a great deal about. But now, everywhere I turn, there are consequences. And they are not like dislocated visions, false seeings. They are real and located and they have context. Like the photograph that Selena is giving to me now. A photograph of a woman on a beach wrapped inside sorrow, wrapped inside herself. I don't recognise the woman because she is no longer me.

'We could do a ceremonial burning,' Selena says, solemnly.

I laugh. 'I think I've been through enough cathartic acts since yesterday.'

'What're you going to do now?' She smiles and says, optimism as ever intact, 'Maybe Jason'll zoom in on a speedboat, run across the sand and sweep you up in his arms.' She laughs. 'Except we're not in a movie.'

'No.' I pause, touch the sand and think of another, more familiar soil. 'I'm going to have a memorial service for Aurora. In France. At Mémé and Pépé's farm. I'll ask Jason to come.'

Selena is quiet for a moment and then says, 'You should

take the blanket and the other stuff you bought for her. Bury it too.'

'I will.'

'I'm going to buy a kaleidoscope for her. You can take it for me and put it in the ground.'

'Why a kaleidoscope?'

'Because it's like a camera but different. You can change the patterns in a kaleidoscope.'

'Yes.' And then I smile because there will always be a piece of earth holding a blanket and a kaleidoscope, marking the memory of my daughter.

'Good luck, Gaelle.'

'I'll miss you, Selena.'

'I won't miss you—I've met a boy.'

'What! You tell me that now! What boy? Where?'

'Questions, questions.' Selena grins. 'You're as bad as my mum.'

'Well now you'll have to write to me. Fill me in on all the details. And I'll have to write back because it'll be my turn to ask the questions.'

Selena jumps up and wraps her arms around my neck before she runs off, then turns back to call out, 'I'll miss you too.'

Back in my cottage I pick up my phone. And I let my mind stray for just a moment, because not every piece of invention feeds a damaging delusion, and I imagine myself walking towards the farmhouse, no longer a girl in a green dress looking backwards, searching for a creature from a fable. I imagine Mémé and Pépé, faces preserved by love, waiting in the *allée* of lime trees, wrapped in leaves, half-lit by the falling sun. The river, full of winter rain, clattering rocks into smoothness. The air, full of brine and damp and constancy. And a man walking up the hill towards me, beneath indigo strips of approaching dusk. A man who says my name, nothing more.

Now I am ready to find out what will come after. I scroll down to 'home.'

The phone rings. Then it is picked up.

'Hello?' Jason's voice.

'Jason.'

'Gaelle.'

Time to find out if there is some truth after all in the fiction of love.

Acknowledgements

Most of my thanks go to my husband Russell for always believing I would be a writer and that I would publish this book. Thanks also to my daughters, Ruby and Audrey, and to Darcy, who show me every day what it really means to be a mother.

I was lucky enough to win the 2008 T.A.G. Hungerford Award for an early version of this novel and I gratefully acknowledge the award partners—Fremantle Press, Writing WA, New Edition Bookshop and the *West Australian*—for actively seeking out and supporting new writers and new writing in this way.

Julienne van Loon, my wonderful Masters supervisor at Curtin University, was instrumental in helping me grope my way from a collection of scraps to something that resembled a book, as were Maria Papas and Maureen Gibbons from my writing group—thanks for the encouragement and feedback.

Janet Blagg's editorial input was astute and invaluable and I thank her for her time and patience in the process of transforming my manuscript into a novel.

A first draft of the novel was completed while I was

Writer in Residence at the Katharine Susannah Prichard Writers' Centre and with the Fellowship of Australian Writers Western Australia, and I thank both these organisations for the time and space to write the first draft.

Grateful acknowledgement is made to Random House for permission to reprint an excerpt from *Invisible Cities* by Italo Calvino, published by Secker & Warburg, and to Virago, an imprint of Little, Brown Book Group, for permission to reprint an excerpt from Margaret Atwood's poem 'A Paper Bag', taken from *Eating Fire: Selected Poetry 1965–1996*.

ALSO AVAILABLE

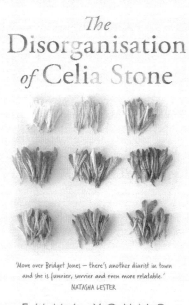

The **Disorganisation** *of* **Celia Stone**

'Move over Bridget Jones — there's another diarist in town
and she is funnier, savvier and even more relatable.'
NATASHA LESTER

EMMA YOUNG

Celia Stone knows that being super-organised is the secret to a successful career, a happy marriage and a bright future—and that with enough discipline, careful planning and hard work, you can retire early and reap the rewards.

But when Jes, her loving, perfect husband, puts an important question to her, all the lists and productivity planners in the world can't help Celia answer it. Will this be the year when Celia can't contain everything in a spreadsheet? Are there some things that can't be controlled at all?

'Move over Bridget Jones—there's another diarist in town and she is funnier, savvier and even more relatable.' *Natasha Lester*

FROM FREMANTLEPRESS.COM.AU

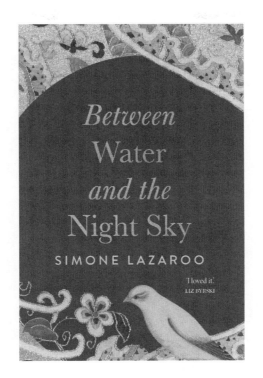

ALSO AVAILABLE

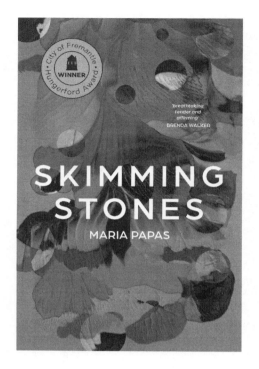

Grace first met her lover, Nate, as a teenager, their bond forged as siblings of cancer patients in hospital corridors and waiting rooms. Now, Grace has chosen nursing because it is a comforting world of science and certainty. But the paediatric ward is also a place of miracles and heartbreak. When faced with a dramatic emergency, Grace is confronted once more with memories of her sister's illness. Heading south to Lake Clifton and the haunts of her childhood, Grace discovers that a stone cast across a lake sends out ripples long after it has sunk from view.

'Elegantly crafted and deeply absorbing ...' *West Australian*

FROM FREMANTLEPRESS.COM.AU

FROM FREMANTLE PRESS

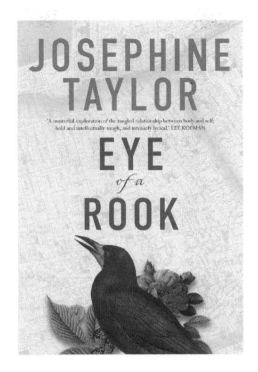

In 1860s London, Arthur sees his wife suddenly struck down by a pain for which Emily can find no words. She is forced to endure harmful treatments and is reliant on him for guidance. Meanwhile, in contemporary Perth, Alice and her husband, Duncan, find their marriage threatened as Alice investigates the history of hysteria, female sexuality and the treatment of the female body—her own and the bodies of those who came before.

'Taylor's style is exquisite, detailed and evocative ... The worlds and women portrayed in this book come alive in a burst of language and imagery ...' *Westerly*

AND ALL GOOD BOOKSTORES

ALSO AVAILABLE

Julia Lambett has been given the job of moving her difficult father out of his home and into care. But when Julia arrives at the 1970s suburban palace of her childhood, she finds her father has adopted a mysterious dog and refuses to leave.

Frustrated in her quest, when childhood friend Davina crosses her path, Julia turns to her for comfort and support. But soon Julia begins to doubt her friend's motivations. Why is Davina taking such a determined interest in all the things that Julia thought she had left behind?

'... a compulsively readable domestic noir ... a great read.' *AU Review*

FROM FREMANTLEPRESS.COM.AU

Falling pregnant was not on the agenda when Simone moved to London to start a career. Even though she's only known her boyfriend Paul for a year, and his apartment is hardly suitable to raise a child, she's determined to be a good mother.

When Paul's cousin Rachel turns up, it should be a godsend. But there's something about her that Simone doesn't trust. Fighting sleep deprivation and a rising sense of unease, Simone begins to question Rachel's motives and wonder what secrets are being kept from her.

'... a slick domestic psychological thriller with a hint of *The Girl on the Train* about it.' *Writing WA*

First published 2010 by
FREMANTLE PRESS

This edition first published 2023.

Fremantle Press Inc. trading as Fremantle Press
PO Box 158, North Fremantle, Western Australia, 6159
fremantlepress.com.au

Cover images: Alexey Kazantsev / Trevillion Images, trevillion.com
Diego PH on Unsplash, unsplash.com and iStock, istockphoto.com
Designed by Nada Backovic, nadabackovic.com
Printed and bound by IPG

A catalogue record for this
book is available from the
National Library of Australia

NATIONAL
LIBRARY
OF AUSTRALIA

ISBN 9781760992477 (paperback)
ISBN 9781760992484 (ebook)

Department of
Local Government, Sport
and Cultural Industries
GOVERNMENT OF
WESTERN AUSTRALIA

lotterywest

Fremantle Press is supported by the State Government through the
Department of Local Government, Sport and Cultural Industries.

Fremantle Press respectfully acknowledges the Whadjuk people of
the Noongar nation as the Traditional Owners and Custodians of the
land where we work in Walyalup.